Biloxi Blues

A NEW COMEDY

by Neil Simon

SAMUEL FRENCH, INC.

45 WEST 25TH STREET   NEW YORK 10010
7623 SUNSET BOULEVARD   HOLLYWOOD 90046
LONDON   *TORONTO*

IMPORTANT PRODUCTION NOTE

The text of BILOXI BLUES makes reference to several songs. Producers are hereby cautioned that permission to produce the Play *does not* include permission to use *any* of this material in production. Producers ought to procure permission to use this material from the copyright owners.

BILLING AND CREDIT REQUIREMENTS

All producers of BILOXI BLUES must give credit to the Author in all programs and in all instances in which the title of the Play appears for purposes of advertising, publicizing or otherwise exploiting the Play and/or production. The author's name must appear on a separate line in which no other name appears, immediately following the title of the play, and must appear in size of type not less than fifty percent the size of title type.

CAST

(in order of appearance)

Roy Selridge	BRIAN TARANTINA
Joseph Wykowski	MATT MULHERN
Don Carney	ALAN RUCK
Eugene Morris Jerome	MATTHEW BRODERICK
Arnold Epstein	BARRY MILLER
Sgt. Merwin J. Toomey	BILL SADLER
James Hennesey	GEOFFREY SHARP
Rowena	RANDALL EDWARDS
Daisy Hannigan	PENELOPE ANN MILLER

STANDBYS

Standbys never substitute for a listed player unless a specific
announcement is made at the time of the performance.

For Eugene — GEOFFREY SHARP, GREG GERMANN; for Selridge and Wykowski —
WOODY HARRELSON; for Carney and Hennesey—JIM FYFE; for Epstein—GREG GER-
MANN; for Sgt. Toomey—JAMEY SHERIDAN; for Rowena—JOAN GOODFELLOW;
for Daisy—JOYCE O'BRIEN.

4

NEIL SIMON THEATRE
UNDER THE DIRECTION OF THE MESSRS. NEDERLANDER

Emanuel Azenberg
in association with Center Theatre Group/Ahmanson Theatre Los Angeles
presents

Matthew Broderick
in
Neil Simon's

with

Bill Sadler   Barry Miller

Randall Edwards   **Penelope Ann Miller**
Matt Mulhern   **Alan Ruck**
Geoffrey Sharp   **Brian Tarantina**

Setting Designed by   Costumes Designed by   Lighting Designed by
David Mitchell   **Ann Roth**   **Tharon Musser**

Directed by
Gene Saks

TO MY GRANDSON,
ANDREW LELAND

Biloxi Blues

ACT ONE

*The coach of an old railroad train, pressed into service
because of the war.*
It is 1943.
*(All set pieces are representational, stylized and free-
flowing. We have a lot of territory to cover here . . .)*
*Four soldiers, dressed in fatigues, from eighteen to twenty
years old, are stretched out across the coach seats,
facing each other, their legs reaching out onto the
opposite seats. Three of the soldiers are sleeping.
They are JOSEPH WYKOWSKI, ROY SELRIDGE
and DON CARNEY. The fourth boy is EUGENE
MORRIS JEROME. He is awake and sitting up,
writing in a school notebook. It is quiet except for
the rumbling of the train along the tracks. A fifth
boy, ARNOLD EPSTEIN, sleeps in the baggage
rack above the others.*
*It is night and a single light illuminates the group. ROY,
in an effort to get more comfortable, turns and his
shoeless foot crawls practically into WYKOWSKI's
mouth. WYKOWSKI, annoyed, slaps ROY's foot
away.*

SELRIDGE. (*waking*) Hey! What the hell's with you?
WYKOWSKI. Get your foot out of my mouth, horse-
face.
SELRIDGE. Up your keester with a meathook, Kowski.
CARNEY. Knock it off, pissheads.
WYKOWSKI. Go take a flying dump, Carney.

7

CARNEY. Yeah. In your mother's hairnet, homo! (*They all return to sleeping.*)

EUGENE. (*aloud to audience*) . . . It was my fourth day in the army and so far I hated everyone . . . We were on a filthy train riding from Fort Dix, New Jersey to Biloxi, Mississippi and in three days nobody washed. The aroma was murder. We were supposed to be fighting Germany and Japan but instead we were stinking up America. (*The train rumbles along . . . ROY peers out the window.*)

SELRIDGE. Where the hell are we? (*EUGENE is still engrossed in his writing. ROY kicks him.*) Hey! Shakespeare! Where the hell are we?

EUGENE. West Virginia.

SELRIDGE. No shit? . . . Where's that near?

EUGENE. You don't know where West Virginia is? Didn't you ever take Geography?

SELRIDGE. I was sick that day.

EUGENE. You don't know what part of the country it's in?

SELRIDGE. (*rises, grabs crotch*) Yeah. *This* part. Up yours, Jerome.

EUGENE. (*reads what he has written*) Roy Selridge from Schenectady, New York smelled like a tuna fish sandwich left out in the rain. He thought he had a terrific sense of humor but it was hard to laugh at a guy who had cavities in nineteen out of thirty-two teeth. (*The train rumbles on.*)

WYKOWSKI. (*opens his eyes*) Jesus Christ! Who did that?

EUGENE. What?

WYKOWSKI. Someone let one go! . . . Holy Jeez. (*fans his cap in front of his face*) I need a gas mask . . . (*lights *a match*) You writing all this stuff in your diary? "Major fart in West Virginia."

EUGENE. It's not a diary. It's my memoirs.

WYKOWSKI. Well, you don't have to write it down because *that* one will stay in your book forever . . . Whoo! Jeez! (*He goes back to sleep.*)

EUGENE. (*to audience*) Joseph Wykowski from Bridgeport, Connecticut had two interesting characteristics. He had the stomach of a goat and could eat anything. His favorite was Hershey bars with the wrappers still on it . . . The other peculiar trait was that he had a permanent erection. I'm talking about night and day, during marching or sleeping. There's no explaining this phenomena unless he has a unique form of paralysis. (*The train rumbles on in the night.*)

CARNEY. (*His eyes are closed and he suddenly starts to sing a lively song of the period with practically full voice.*)

WYKOWSKI. Wake him up! Wake him up, for crise sakes! (*ROY kicks CARNEY in the chest with his foot. CARNEY jumps.*)

CARNEY. What the hell's wrong with you?

SELRIDGE. It's two-thirty in the God damn morning. You were singing again.

CARNEY. I was not.

SELRIDGE. What do you mean, "You was not"? You practically made a record.

CARNEY. What was I singing?

SELRIDGE. "Chattanooga Choo-Choo."

CARNEY. I don't even know the words to "Chattanooga Choo-Choo."

WYKOWSKI. Maybe not awake. But you know them when you're sleeping.

CARNEY. (*to EUGENE*) Hey, Gene. Was I singing "Chattanooga Choo-Choo"?

EUGENE. Yeah.

CARNEY. . . . Was I good?

EUGENE. Well, for a guy who was sleeping, it wasn't bad.

CARNEY. Damn. I wish I heard it.

EUGENE. (*to audience*) Donald Carney from Montclair, New Jersey was an okay guy until someone made the fatal mistake of telling him he sounded like Perry Como. His voice was flat but his sister wasn't. She had the biggest breasts I ever saw. She came to visit him at Fort Dix wearing a tight red sweater and that's when I first discovered Wykowski's condition. (*The train rumbles on.*)

WYKOWSKI. (*sits up*) God damn it. Someone let go again . . . Was it you, Carney?

CARNEY. I was singing, wasn't I? I'm not going to do that while I'm singing.

WYKOWSKI. Yeah? Well, maybe you sang to cover it up.

SELRIDGE. Wait a minute. Wait a minute. (*He looks up.*) It's coming from up there. (*They all look up. EPSTEIN has been sleeping on the grilling of the baggage rack with his rear end to the audience. WYKOWSKI whacks his cap hard against EPSTEIN's butt.*)

WYKOWSKI. Hey! Bombardier! Kill Germans, not G.I.s. (*EPSTEIN turns around. He is slight of build.*)

EPSTEIN. I'm sorry. I'm not feeling very well.

SELRIDGE. Yeah? Well, now we're *all* not feeling very well.

EUGENE. Leave him alone. He didn't do it on purpose.

SELRIDGE. (*to EPSTEIN*) You hear, Epstein? He's

your buddy. Aim the next one at him, okay?

EPSTEIN. Does anyone have an Alka-Seltzer tablet?

WYKOWSKI. Plugging it up ain't gonna help, Epstein. (*He and ROY laugh. They all go back to their sleeping positions.*)

EUGENE. (*stops writing, looks at audience*) Arnold Epstein of Queens Boulevard, New York was a sensitive, well read, intelligent young man. His major flaw was that he was incapable of digesting food stronger than hard boiled eggs . . . I didn't think he'd last long in the army because during wartime it's very hard to go home for dinner every night . . . (*The train rumbles on.*) Hey, Arnold! What's the best book you ever read?

EPSTEIN. *War and Peace* . . . The fifth time.

EUGENE. If I wanted to become a writer, who do you recommend I read?

EPSTEIN. The entire third floor of the New York Public Library.

WYKOWSKI. Hey, Epstein? Can you read lips? Read this! (*Bronx cheer; SELRIDGE laughs.*)

EUGENE. (*to audience*) If the Germans only knew what was coming over, they would be looking forward to this invasion . . . I'm Eugene Morris Jerome of Brighton Beach, Brooklyn, New York and you can tell I've never been away from home before. In my duffel bag are twelve pot roast sandwiches my mother gave me . . . There were three things I was determined to do in this war. Become a writer, not get killed and lose my virginity . . . But first I had to get through basic training in the murky swamps of Mississippi . . . (*Silence for a moment, then CARNEY, eyes closed, sings a popular song of the period.*)

(*Lights dim as the train rumbles on. As CARNEY's sing-*

ing slowly fades, we hear the sound of men march-
ing and chanting out the cadence rhythms so famil-
iar in the military.
Lights come up in the barracks as the sound of march-
ing men fades.
EUGENE, WYKOWSKI, EPSTEIN, SELRIDGE and
CARNEY amble into the barracks carrying their
heavy barracks bags. They are hot, sweaty and tired.
They look around at their new "home" for the next
few months.)

EUGENE. Boy, it's hot. This is hot! I am really hot!
Oh, God, is it hot! (*puts duffel in a lower bunk*)
WYKOWSKI. You can cool off on the top 'cause that's
my bunk down there. (*He throws EUGENE's duffel on*
top and throws his own on the lower. EPSTEIN throws
his duffel on the top bunk next to EUGENE. He looks
at the rolled up mattress and picks off a bedbug. They
have all put their duffels on bunks and sit or lie down.)
CARNEY. I'm so tired I'm just gonna sleep on the
springs.
EUGENE. It never got this hot in Brooklyn. This is like
Africa hot. *Tarzan* couldn't take this kind of hot.
SELRIDGE. Where's the phone? Call the manager.
There's no ice water.

(*SGT. TOOMEY enters with clipboard.*)

TOOMEY. Dee-tail, attenSHUN!! (*The boys slowly get*
to their feet.)
SELRIDGE. Hi, Sarge.
TOOMEY. I think it's in your best interests, men, to
move your asses when I yell ATTENSHUN!! MOVE
IT!!! I want a single line right there! (*They all jump and*

line up in front of their bunks. TOOMEY paces up and down the line, looking them over.) Until the order "At Ease," is given, gentlemen, you are not "At Ease," is that understood? 'Tenshun! (*They snap to attention. He looks at them a moment.*) At Ease! (*They stand "At Ease" . . . TOOMEY looks them over, then consults his clipboard.*) Answer when your name is called. The answer to that question is Ho. Not yes, not here, not right, not sir or any other unacceptable form of reply except the aforementioned Ho, am I understood? Wykowski, Joseph T.

WYKOWSKI. Ho!

TOOMEY. Selridge, Roy W.

ROY. Ho!

TOOMEY. Carney, Donald J.

CARNEY. Ho!

TOOMEY. Jerome, Eugene M.

EUGENE. Ho!

TOOMEY. Epstein, Arnold B.

EPSTEIN. Ho Ho! (*TOOMEY looks at him.*)

TOOMEY. Are there two Arnold Epsteins in this company?

EPSTEIN. No, Sergeant.

TOOMEY. Then just give me one God damn Ho.

EPSTEIN. Yes, Sergeant.

TOOMEY. Epstein, Arnold B.

EPSTEIN. Ho!

TOOMEY. One more time.

EPSTEIN. Ho!

TOOMEY. Let me hear it again.

EPSTEIN. Ho!

TOOMEY. Am I understood?

EPSTEIN. Ho! (*as if saying "yes"*)

EUGENE. (*to audience*) Arnold Epstein was the worst

soldier in World War Two and that included the deserters
. . . He just refused to show respect to those he thought
were his intellectual inferiors.

TOOMEY. (*to men*) . . . My name is Toomey. Sergeant
Merwin J. Toomey and I am in charge of C Company
during your ten weeks of basic training here in Beautiful
Biloxi, Mississippi, after which those of you who have
survived the heat, humidity, roaches, spiders, snakes,
dry rot, fungus, dysentery, syphilis, gonorrhea and tick
fever, will be sent to some shit island in the Pacific or
some turd pile in Northern Sicily. In either case, return-
ing to your mommas and poppas with your balls intact
is highly improbable. There's only one way to come out
of a war healthy of body and sane of mind and that way
is to be born the favorite daughter of the President of
the United States . . . I speak from experience having
served fourteen months in the North African campaign
where seventy-three per cent of my comrades are buried
under the sand of an A-rab desert. The colorful ribbons
on my chest will testify to the fact that my government is
grateful for my contribution having donated a small
portion of my brains to this conflict, the other portion
being protected by a heavy steel plate in my head. This
injury has caused me to become a smart, compassionate,
understanding and sympathetic teacher of raw, young
men — or the cruelest, craziest, most sadistic God damn
son of a bitch you ever saw . . . and that's something you
won't know until ten weeks from now, do I make myself
clear, Epstein?

ARNOLD. I think so.

TOOMEY. DO I MAKE MYSELF CLEAR, EPSTEIN??

ARNOLD. *Ho!*

TOOMEY. DO I MAKE MYSELF CLEAR, JEROME?

EUGENE. Ho yes!

TOOMEY. Ho *what*?

EUGENE. Ho nothing.

TOOMEY. God damn right, boy.

EUGENE. (*to audience*) I hated the lousy movies. I thought I was going to get a nice officer like James Stewart.

TOOMEY. (*looks at EUGENE*) Are you paying attention to me, Jerome?

EUGENE. (*nervously*) Yes ho. I mean Ho, sir. Just plain Ho.

TOOMEY. Where are you from, Jerome?

EUGENE. 1427 Pulaski Avenue.

TOOMEY. In my twelve years in the army, I never met one God damn dogface who came from 1427 Pulaski Avenue. Why is that, Jerome?

EUGENE. Because it's my home. Only one family lives there. I'm sorry. I meant I live in Brighton Beach, Brooklyn, New York. (*TOOMEY notices EPSTEIN shifting from foot to foot.*)

TOOMEY. Hey, Fred Astaire! You trying to tell me something?

ARNOLD. I have to go to the bathroom, Sergeant.

TOOMEY. Now how are you going to do that? We don't have bathrooms in the army.

ARNOLD. They had them in Fort Dix.

TOOMEY. Not bathrooms, they didn't.

ARNOLD. Yes, they did, Sergeant. I went in them a lot.

TOOMEY. Well, I'm telling you we don't have any bathrooms on this base. Do you doubt my veracity?

ARNOLD. No, Sergeant.

TOOMEY. Then you've got a problem, haven't you, Epstein?

ARNOLD. Ho ho.

TOOMEY. You bet your ass, ho ho . . . Do you know why you've got a problem, Epstein?

ARNOLD. Because I have to go real bad.

TOOMEY. No, son. You've got a problem because you don't know army terminology. The place where a U.S. soldier goes to defecate, relieve himself, open his bowels, shit, fart, dump, crap and unload is called the latrine. La-trine! (*EUGENE smiles.*) Want to tell us what's funny about that, Jerome?

EUGENE. Well . . . that you said all those words in one sentence.

TOOMEY. That's why these ribbons are pinned on my shirt. Because I'm an experienced army man. Do you understand that, Jerome?

EUGENE. Ha.

TOOMEY. What?

EUGENE. Ho.

TOOMEY. Where are you from, Wykowski?

WYKOWSKI. Bridgeport, Connecticut.

TOOMEY. Do you know where that is, Selridge?

SELRIDGE. It's er . . . in Connecticut. Bridgeport, I think.

TOOMEY. Is that right, Wykowski?

WYKOWSKI. Ho.

TOOMEY. (*looks directly at ROY*) And what did you do in Bridgeport, soldier?

SELRIDGE. I was never there, Sergeant.

TOOMEY. I wasn't talking to you, Selridge.

SELRIDGE. Oh. You were looking at me.

TOOMEY. I may be looking at you but I am talking to the soldier from Bridgeport. (*looks into ROY's face*) Now what did you do there, Wykowski? (*They all look confused.*)

WYKOWSKI. I drove a truck. A moving van. I was a

furniture mover.

TOOMEY. That's just what they need in the South Pacific, Wykowski. Someone who knows how to move furniture around in the jungle. (*EPSTEIN half raises hand.*) I believe Private Epstein has a question.

ARNOLD. May I go to the latrine, Sergeant?

TOOMEY. No. I am addressing the new members of my company, Epstein. (*looks directly into WYKOWSKI's face*) What's your name again, soldier?

WYKOWSKI. Wykowski.

TOOMEY. I am talking to the man next to you.

SELRIDGE. Selridge!

TOOMEY. (*points to CARNEY*) *You*, boy! You are the one I am directing my question to.

CARNEY. Carney, sir. Donald J . . . Ho!

TOOMEY. I didn't ask if you were here. I can *see* that you're here. I asked where you're from, Carney, Donald J.

CARNEY. I don't remember . . . Er, Montclair, New Jersey.

TOOMEY. And what was your civilian occupation in Montclair, New Jersey, Private Carney, Donald J.?

CARNEY. I didn't have any.

TOOMEY. No occupation? You were unemployed then, is that right?

CARNEY. No, Sergeant. I worked in a shoe store. In the stock room.

TOOMEY. (*stares at him*) Did I not hear you just say you didn't have an occupation?

CARNEY. Not in Montclair. I *lived* in Montclair. I worked in Teaneck. You just asked what my occupation was in Montclair.

TOOMEY. I see . . . Is it your intention, Private Carney, Donald J., to humiliate and ridicule me in front of my company?

CARNEY. No, Sergeant.

TOOMEY. And yet that is precisely what you did. As I stand here in front of my newly arrived company, you took this opportunity, assuming that because of my Southern heritage, I was an uneducated and illiterate cotton picker, you purposefully and deliberately humiliated me. Did you think for one second you would get away with that, Private Carney, Donald J.? . . .

CARNEY. I wasn't trying to get away with . . .

TOOMEY. Well, I can assure you, YOU DID NOT AND WILL NOT! You just got your ass in a sling, boy! *Does everyone understand that?*

ALL. (*together*) Ho!

TOOMEY. What?

ALL. (*together*) *HO!!!*

TOOMEY. I am, strictly speaking, Carney, old army. And old army means discipline. Can you do push-ups, Private Carney?

CARNEY. Yes, Sergeant.

TOOMEY. What is the highest total of push-ups you ever achieved in one session, Private Carney?

CARNEY. I'm not too strong in the arms. About ten . . . maybe fifteen.

TOOMEY. Congratulations, Carney. You are about to break your old record. I want one hundred push-ups from you, Carney, and I want them *now*. AM I UNDERSTOOD?

CARNEY. One hundred? Oh, I couldn't possibly do one hu—

TOOMEY. HIT THE FLOOR, SOLDIER!!!

CARNEY. I could do, say, twenty a day for five days—

TOOMEY. Count off, God dammit and move your ass!

CARNEY. (*starts doing push-ups*) One . . . two . . . three . . . four . . . five . . .

TOOMEY. (*looks into EPSTEIN's eyes*) Nobody eats,

drinks, sleeps or goes to the latrine until I hear one hundred.

CARNEY. Six . . . seven . . . Oh, God . . . nine . . . ten . . .

TOOMEY. Eight. You forgot eight, didn't you, boy?

CARNEY. I did it. I just didn't say it.

TOOMEY. Well, say them all, Donny boy. Let's start again from one. Let's hear it.

CARNEY. One . . . two . . . three . . . (*CARNEY continues this throughout the scene with great difficulty.*)

TOOMEY. (*shouts*) *Private Jerome!* Do you think this is cruel, unfair and unjust punishment being inflicted on Private Carney?

EUGENE. Oh, gee, I don't know. It's my first day—

TOOMEY. I want the God Almighty truth from you. Is this punishment unfair and unjust, Private Jerome?

EUGENE. (*to audience*) If only I had a heart murmur, I wouldn't be in this trouble.

TOOMEY. Your answer, boy.

EUGENE. Well, I think it was a misunderstanding . . . I think er—(*feels his head*) I think I have swamp fever, sir.

TOOMEY. Yes or no, Jerome. Am I being unfair to the young man who is breaking his ass on the floor?

EUGENE. In my opinion? . . . Yes, Sergeant.

TOOMEY. I see . . . Apparently, Jerome, you don't understand the benefits of discipline. It is discipline that will win this war for us. Therefore, until you learn it, soldier, I will just have to keep teaching it to you . . . *Selridge!* One hundred push-ups. *Hit* the floor!

SELRIDGE. Me??? . . . I didn't say nothin'.

TOOMEY. When we do battle, we are sometimes called upon to sacrifice ourselves for the sake of others.

SELRIDGE. Yeah, but we didn't do battle yet.

TOOMEY. ON YOUR FACE, SOLDIER!!

SELRIDGE. (*on floor*) One . . . two . . . three . . . four . . . (*They continue.*)

TOOMEY. (*to EUGENE*) What I have done to Private Selridge may seem even more unfair and unjust than what I did to Private Carney. Is that your opinion, Private Jerome?

EUGENE. (*takes a deep breath*) . . . No, Sergeant.

TOOMEY. Hold it, boys. (*To others; they stop.*) You all heard that. Private Jerome approves of my method of discipline. He thinks what I am doing is fair, moral and just. Therefore, with his approval and endorsement, Private Wykowski will join us for one hundred push-ups. Hit the deck, Wykowski! I can see how grateful you are. You can thank your buddy, Private Jerome.

WYKOWSKI. (*glares at EUGENE*) I will. Later. (*starts push-ups*)

TOOMEY. Back to work, boys.

WYKOWSKI. One . . . two . . . three . . . four . . .

EUGENE. (*to WYKOWSKI*) I'm sorry. (*CARNEY is struggling.*)

CARNEY. I—I don't think I can do any more, Sergeant.

TOOMEY. I realize that, son, and I sympathize with you. If only there were some way I could help you.

EUGENE. I could finish it for him, Sergeant.

TOOMEY. That's damn decent of you, Jerome, but I think Private Carney doesn't expect other men to shoulder his responsibility.

CARNEY. I would be willing to make an exception, Sergeant.

TOOMEY. What I think you need, Carney, is inspiration. Therefore, I am asking volunteers to join Privates Carney, Selridge and Wykowski on the barracks floor. All volunteers take one step forward and shout, "Ho!" Sound off!

EUGENE. (*takes one step forward*) Ho! (*ARNOLD remains silent and doesn't move.*)

TOOMEY. We have one volunteer . . . and one inconclusive. (*He crosses to ARNOLD, moves in face to face.*) Does your silence mean you are not volunteering, Private Epstein?

ARNOLD. I have a slight deformity of the spine which escaped the medical exam—

TOOMEY. ON YOUR FACE, EPSTEIN!!! (*ARNOLD drops to floor.*) Ready . . . Ho!

ARNOLD. One . . . two . . . three . . . four . . . (*All four men are doing push-ups. CARNEY and EPSTEIN struggle the most. TOOMEY paces back and forth, nodding happily.*)

TOOMEY. Now we're moving ahead in our quest for discipline . . . As the sweat pours off your brows and your puny muscles strain to lift your flabby, chubby, jellied bodies, think of Private Jerome of Brighton Beach, New York, who is *not* down there beside you. *Not* sharing your pain, *not* sharing your struggle . . . Fate always chooses someone to get a free ride. The kind of man who always gets away with all kinds of shit. In this company it seems to be Private Eugene M. Jerome. Eventually we get to hate those men. Hate them, loathe them and despise them. How does Private Jerome learn to deal with this cold wall of anger and hostility? By learning to endure it alone. That, gentlemen, is the supreme lesson in discipline. You're slowing down, boys. The sooner you finish, the sooner you'll get to our fine Southern cooking . . . Up down . . . Up down . . . Carry on instructions, Jerome. Up down . . . up down . . . (*TOOMEY leaves.*)

EUGENE. (*to audience*) It was then I decided I had to get out of the army . . . I thought of shooting off a part of my body I might not need in later life but I couldn't find any . . . But the worst was still to come . . .

(*Lights out on EUGENE.*

*Lights up on section of mess hall. WYKOWSKI, SEL-
    RIDGE, CARNEY and EPSTEIN are sitting at a
    wooden table, staring frozen faced at the aluminum
    tray filled with "supper" in front of them. Nobody
    moves. The forks in their hands are raised motion-
    less above the tray.*)

CARNEY. What do you think it is?

WYKOWSKI. My brother had this in the marines. It's
S.O.S.

CARNEY. What's S.O.S.?

WYKOWSKI. Shit on a shingle.

CARNEY. (*looks at it*) Yeah, that's what it looks like
alright.

SELRIDGE. What do you mean? They take a shingle
and they put — shit on it?

WYKOWSKI. It's beef. Creamed chipped beef.

ARNOLD. Why would you chip something after it's
been creamed?

WYKOWSKI. It doesn't look so bad to me. Hell, I'm
hungry. (*He takes a forkful and eats it. They all watch
him.*) . . . It's terrific . . . It needs ketchup, that's all.
(*He puts ketchup on it.*)

SELRIDGE. They oughta drop this stuff over Germany.
The whole country would come out with their hands up.
(*EUGENE appears, carrying his tray. His mouth is
agape, his face aghast as he looks at what's on his tray.*)

EUGENE. I saw this in the Bronx Zoo. The gorillas
were throwing it at each other.

ARNOLD. If you can't eat this, you can get something
else. It's government regulations. Enlisted men must be
served palatable food.

WYKOWSKI. Why don't you ask them for some matzoh

ball soup, Epstein. I hear the army makes great matzoh ball soup. (*He and SELRIDGE laugh. EUGENE looks emphatically at ARNOLD.*)

ARNOLD. It's my right to speak up. (*He looks around.*) I'm going to speak to the sergeant.

CARNEY. Sit down, would you, please?

EUGENE. Don't start in with him, Arnold. He's crazy. This was probably his recipe.

WYKOWSKI. (*to EUGENE and ARNOLD*) Listen, you two guys. Don't give the sergeant any more crap. 'Cause when he doesn't like you, he doesn't like the rest of us. Any guy who screws up in this platoon is in deep shit with me, understand?

ARNOLD. Who made you Lieutenant Colonel?

WYKOWSKI. *I* did. I promoted myself. If I have to do any more push-ups account of you, Epstein, you're going to be underneath me when I'm doing them.

SELRIDGE. Well, now we know who the fruits are. (*He laughs.*)

ARNOLD. I'm not even supposed to be in the army with my stomach. No one's going to make me eat this if I don't want to.

(*JAMES HENNESEY, a soldier their own age, on KP, crosses to refill their sugar jars.*)

HENNESEY. You guys hear what happened over at Baker Company? Some kid went nuts. Said he was going home, didn't want no part of this army. An officer tried to stop him and the kid belted him one, broke the Captain's nose. They said this guy's sure to get five to ten years in Leavenworth. They don't crap around in the army, you find that out real fast.

CARNEY. I hope they ship us out to the Pacific. At least we'd get Chinese food.

HENNESEY. My name is Hennesey. I'm in your platoon. They gave me eight straight days of KP.

WYKOWSKI. How come?

HENNESEY. I left over two spoonfuls of barley soup. Two lousy spoonfuls . . . Be careful, you guys. (*He turns and moves away quickly as SGT. TOOMEY crosses to table.*)

TOOMEY. How my boys doing? (*All except EPSTEIN smile and greet him warmly.*) How's the chow?

WYKOWSKI. (*overly cheerful*) First rate, Sarge.

SELRIDGE. They don't give you enough.

EUGENE. Surprisingly interesting food, Sarge.

TOOMEY. Not hungry, Epstein?

ARNOLD. I find enough nourishment in bread and water, Sergeant.

TOOMEY. Well, you're all going to need plenty of nourishment with ten back breaking weeks ahead of us, starting tonight.

CARNEY. Tonight?

TOOMEY. Worked out a little surprise for you. Something to work off tonight's dinner. We're going on a midnight hike, men.

EUGENE. Midnight?

TOOMEY. Not too far, this being your first night in camp. Just a short fifteen mile walk around the marshes and swamps. How does that sound to you, Jerome? You think that's a reasonable request of me to make?

EUGENE. We've sort of elected Wykowski our leader. I think he should answer that. (*WYKOWSKI glares at EUGENE.*)

TOOMEY. Is that right, Wykowski?

WYKOWSKI. I don't question orders, Sergeant. I just follow them.

TOOMEY. That's a good answer, Wykowski. It's a chicken-shit one, but a good answer . . . How about you, Epstein? You up to a fifteen mile walk around the swamp?

ARNOLD. . . . No, Sergeant.

TOOMEY. No??? Epstein's not up to it, men . . . Why is that, Epstein?

ARNOLD. We've been on a train for five days and five nights. We haven't had one good night's sleep since we left Fort Dix.

TOOMEY. I see . . . Okay. Fair enough, Epstein . . . You're excused from the hike. I appreciate a man who speaks up.

ARNOLD. Thank you, Sergeant.

TOOMEY. You get a good night's sleep just as soon as you've washed, scrubbed and shined every john, urinal and basin in the latrine. If it doesn't sparkle when we get back, then Wykowski and Selridge are going to do two hundred push-ups. That'll put you in good with the boys, Epstein . . . Anyone else care to stay home for the evening? . . . Okay then, let's get moving. Full field packs in front of barracks at twenty-four hundred hours, ready to march. LET'S GET CRACKING! (*They all jump up, except EPSTEIN.*) *HOLD ON ONE GOD DAMN MINUTE!!!* (*They all stop.*) Nobody—but NOBODY—leaves here with good U.S. Army chow untouched, uneaten and unfinished. You can sit there poking at it with your fork till it sprouts weeds, but by God, you will sit there until that tray is empty . . . Line up in front of me, trays extended for inspection. (*They quickly line up in front of TOOMEY in single file. WYKOWSKI is first. TOOMEY looks into his tray.*) Okay, Wykowski, move! (*SEL-RIDGE is next.*) Right, Selridge, move. (*He follows WYKOWSKI out. CARNEY is next. His food is untouched.*) Something wrong with your dinner, Carney?

CARNEY. Yes, Sarge. It's the first food I was ever afraid of.

TOOMEY. You'll like it about a month from now 'cause that's how long you'll be sitting there. Back to your seat! (*CARNEY glumly goes back and sits at the table. EUGENE steps in front of TOOMEY, tray extended.*) Don't approve of our *cuisine*, Jerome?

EUGENE. It's not that, Sarge. It's a religious objection. This is the week that my people fast for two days.

TOOMEY. This is March, Jerome. Rosh-Ahonah and Yom Kippur are in September. I have an all-religion calendar in my barracks room. Don't you try that shit on me again!

EUGENE. It's a different holiday. It's called El Malaguena.

TOOMEY. El Malaguena??

EUGENE. It's for Spanish Jews.

TOOMEY. Carney!

CARNEY. Yes, Sarge?

TOOMEY. Put half your tray on to Jerome's.

CARNEY. (*smiles*) Yes, Sergeant.

TOOMEY. (*to EUGENE*) Eat in good health, Jerome, and Happy El Malaguena to you. (*EUGENE sits as CARNEY eagerly scrapes half his tray into EUGENE's. EUGENE, looking miserable, sits. ARNOLD steps in front of TOOMEY.*) Okay, Epstein, what's your story? And don't tell me today is La Coocharacha.

ARNOLD. I have a legitimate excuse, Sergeant. I have a digestive disorder, diagnosed as a nervous stomach.

TOOMEY. Is that right? And how come you passed the army medical examination?

ARNOLD. It only gets nervous while I'm eating food. I wasn't eating food during the examination. I brought a chicken salad sandwich along to show them what happens when it enters the digestive tract . . .

TOOMEY. Are you a psycho, Epstein? You sound like a psycho to me. That's a psycho story.

ARNOLD. (*reaches into breast pocket*) I have a letter from my internist who's on the staff of Mount Sinai Hospital on Fifth Avenue — (*TOOMEY grabs letter from ARNOLD, quickly reads it.*)

TOOMEY. Did you show this to the army medical examining officer?

ARNOLD. Yes, Sergeant.

TOOMEY. What did he say?

ARNOLD. He said don't eat chicken salad sandwiches and then he accepted me.

TOOMEY. Then this letter ain't worth the paper it's written on. (*He tears it up, shreds it over ARNOLD's food.*) I expect to see everything on that tray gone, Epstein, including that letter. The corporal at the door will be watching you. Good appetite, men. (*turns briskly, starts out*) . . . "El Malaguena" . . . (*ARNOLD sits and the three men sit in stony silence.*)

EUGENE. I've got an idea.

CARNEY. Yeah?

EUGENE. We dump it under the table. We'll be gone by the time they find it.

CARNEY. Great idea. But we have to time it right. When no one's looking.

EUGENE. I'll tell you when.

CARNEY. Remember. Timing's everything.

EUGENE. (*looks around*) . . . Okay. *Now!*

(*In unison they lower their trays under the table. They are about to dump it when the voice of the CORPO-RAL calls out.*)

VOICE. (*sharp*) GET THOSE TRAYS BACK ON THE TABLE. (*They bring trays quickly back up.*)

CARNEY. . . . Work on your timing.

ARNOLD. Give it to me.

CARNEY. What?

ARNOLD. I'm not going to eat mine. No point in all of us suffering. Scrape it onto my tray.

EUGENE. You mean it?

ARNOLD. This is lunacy. I'm an intelligent human being. I refuse to capitulate to the lunatics. One day when this war is over, there will be investigations . . . (*to BOYS*) Go on. Give it to me. (*They scrape food onto ARNOLD's tray.*)

CARNEY. I like you, Epstein, but you're weird as hell . . . But I'll tell you one thing. I'm sitting next to you every meal we get. (*He leaves.*)

EUGENE. I could have used you when my mother made lima beans. (*He leaves.*)

ARNOLD. . . . I won't eat slop . . . I won't eat slop . . . I WON'T EAT SLOP! I WON'T EAT SLOP!

EUGENE. (*appears in field equipment*) . . . Arnold didn't eat the slop. They gave him K.P. for five straight days including cleaning the latrines. But that was better than the midnight march through the murky swamps of Mississippi. (*We hear the sound of eerie birds and strange animals. EUGENE looks up.*) The only time I heard strange sounds like that was at Ebbets Field when the Dodgers played . . . Toomey made Wykowski carry me

the whole fifteen miles just so Wykowski would hate me
more . . . But maybe Toomey was right. If nobody obeys
orders, I'll bet we wouldn't have more than twelve or thir-
teen soldiers fighting the war . . . We'd have headlines
like, "Corporal Stanley Leiberman invades Sicily" . . .

(*Lights off on EUGENE. Lights up on barracks. AR-
    NOLD enters from latrine, EUGENE goes to his
    locker.*)

EUGENE. (*continued*) Hey, Arnold, it was incredible.
You missed it. We were in the swamps up to our necks.
There were water snakes and big lizards that crawled up
your pants and swooping swamp birds that swooped
down and went right for your eyeballs . . . What's wrong,
Arnold? . . . Arnold? . . .
    ARNOLD. Leave me alone!
    EUGENE. What is it? Are you sick?
    ARNOLD. Get away from me. You're like all the rest of
them. I hate every God damn one of you.
    EUGENE. Hey, Arnold, I'm your friend. I'm your
buddy. You can talk to me.
    ARNOLD. (*sits up, looks around*) . . . I'm getting out.
I'm leaving in the morning. I'm going to Mexico or Cen-
tral America till after the war . . . I will not be treated like
dirt, like a maggot. I'm not going to help defend a country that won't even defend its own citizens . . . Bastards!
    EUGENE. Because you pulled latrine duty? We all have
to pull latrine duty. You have to adjust . . . It's all a
game, Arnold. Only it's their ball and their rules. And
they know the game better than we do because they've
been playing it since Valley Forge.
    ARNOLD. . . . I was in the latrine alone. I spent four
hours cleaning it, on my hands and knees. It looked bet-

ter than my mother's bathroom at home. Then these two non-coms come in, one was the cook, that three hundred pound guy and some other slob, with cigar butts in their mouths and reeking from beer . . . They come in to pee only instead of using the urinal, they use one of the johns, both peeing in the same one, making circles, figure-eights. Then they start to walk out and I say, "Hey, I just cleaned that. Please flush the johns." And the big one, the cook, says to me, "Up your ass, rookie," or some other really clever remark . . . And I block the doorway and I say, "There's a printed order on the wall signed by Captain Landon stating the regulations that all facilities must be flushed after using" . . . And I'm requesting that they follow regulations, since I was left in charge, and to please flush the facility . . . And the big one says to me, "Suppose you flush it, New York Jew Kike," and I said my ethnic heritage notwithstanding, please flush the facility . . . They look at each other, this half a ton of brainless beef and suddenly rush me, turn me upside down, grab my ankles and — and — and they lowered me by my feet with my head in the toilet, in their filth, their poison . . . all the way until I couldn't breathe . . . then they pulled off my belt and tied my feet on to the ceiling pipes with my head still in their foul waste and tied my hands behind my back with dirty rags, and they left me there, hanging like a pig that was going to be slaughtered . . . I wasn't strong enough to fight back. I couldn't do it alone. No one came to help me . . . Then the pipe broke and I fell to the ground . . . It took me twenty minutes to get myself untied . . . Twenty minutes! . . . But it will take me the rest of my life to wash off my humiliation. I was degraded. I lost my dignity. If I stay, Gene, if they put a gun in my hands, one night, I swear to God, I'll kill them both . . . I'm not a murderer.

I don't want to disgrace my family . . . But I have to get out of here . . . Now do you understand?

EUGENE. But you can't go AWOL. They'll catch you. They have agents all over the world . . . You'll get back at them one day. Don't you believe in justice?

ARNOLD. . . . You're so damn naive, Eugene.

(*WYKOWSKI and SELRIDGE come out of the latrine in their underwear, carrying towels, toothbrushes and toothpaste.*)

WYKOWSKI. (*scratching*) I got a hundred and twelve God damn mosquite bites.

SELRIDGE. (*shivers*) I pulled twelve leeches off me. I pulled one off near my crotch, it wasn't a leech. Maybe I pulled something else off. (*He gets into bed, still shivering. CARNEY and HENNESEY come out in their underwear, towels.*)

CARNEY. I heard a top secret rumor today. I'm not supposed to repeat it.

WYKOWSKI. What is it?

CARNEY. I can get in trouble if it gets out.

WYKOWSKI. No one's gonna talk. What is it?

CARNEY. I hear they're getting ready to invade Europe and Japan on the same day.

HENNESEY. Where'd you hear that?

CARNEY. On the radio. It was one of them small stations.

EUGENE. Why on the same day?

CARNEY. Surprise attack. You hit them both at dawn. Then they don't have enough time to warn each other.

EUGENE. Hey, Carney. When it's dawn in Europe, it's a day later in Japan. They don't have dawn at the same time. Japan could read about it in their newspapers.

HENNESEY. Besides, we're not ready. We don't have enough trained men to invade both places on the same day.

ARNOLD. You know what *Time* magazine estimates the casualty rate of a full scale invasion would be? Sixty-eight per cent. Sixty-eight per cent of us would be killed or wounded.

WYKOWSKI. No shit? . . . So out of this group, how many is that?

ARNOLD. Of the six of us here, about four point three of us would get it.

CARNEY. What part of your body is point three?

SELRIDGE. Hey, Wykowski. We know what part of *your* body is point three. (*He giggles.*)

EUGENE. Listen, if you knew you were one of the guys who wasn't coming back, if you knew it right now, what would you do with the last few days of your life? It could be anything you want . . . I give everyone five seconds to think about it.

CARNEY. I thought about it. I'm not dying. You think I'm gonna kill myself to entertain *you*?

EUGENE. Why not? It's like a fantasy. I'm giving you the opportunity to do anything in the world you ever dreamed of . . . Come on.

SELRIDGE. I think it's a good idea. Let's play for money.

HENNESEY. For *money*?

SELRIDGE. Yeah. Five bucks a man. The guy with the best fantasy collects the pot.

HENNESEY. That's morbid.

WYKOWSKI. Okay, I'm in. We need a judge.

EUGENE. I'll be the judge.

WYKOWSKI. Why you?

EUGENE. Because I thought of the game. Ante up, everyone. Come on, Hennesey. (*They all put up money except EPSTEIN.*) Come on, Arnold. I *know* you have some great fantasies.

EPSTEIN. I don't sell my fantasies.

WYKOWSKI. Burn his bunk!

EUGENE. Come on, Arnold . . . for me.

SELRIDGE. I love this. I'm gonna clean up.

EUGENE. (*jubilant*) Okay, Carney. You're first. You're dead. Killed in action . . . What would you do with your last days on earth?

CARNEY. How much time do I have to do it in?

EUGENE. A week.

SELRIDGE. I need ten days.

EUGENE. It's my game. You only get a week . . . What would you do with it, Donny?

CARNEY. (*thinks*) Okay . . . I would sing at the Radio City Music Hall. Five shows a day, my own spot. In the audience are four thousand girls and one man. Every girl is gorgeous. Every girl is size 38-24-36 . . . And they all want me . . . real bad.

HENNESEY. Who's the man?

CARNEY. The President of Decca Records. He wants me too. I have a choice. After the last show, I could have all four thousand girls . . . or a contract with Decca Records.

HENNESEY. Which one do you take?

SELRIDGE. (*urging him on*) The record contract. I would take the record contract.

CARNEY. Right. I take the record contract.

SELRIDGE. (*laughs*) MORON!! He believed me. He could have humped four thousand girls and now he's got a record contract that ain't worth shit.

CARNEY. Wrong! Because now I'm a big star and stars get all the girls they want anyway.

SELRIDGE. Yeah? How? You're dead. Girls never go

out with dead record stars.

CARNEY. Bullshit! I paid five bucks for my fantasy. I can do what I want . . . What's my score, Gene?

EUGENE. Well, you started off with an A-minus but you finished with a B.

CARNEY. B. Not bad—better than I ever did in school.

EUGENE. Alright. Selridge is next.

SELRIDGE. Okay . . . Here we go . . . I make it with the seven richest women in the world. And I'm so hot, each dame gives me a million bucks. And at the end of a week, I got seven million bucks. Pretty good, heh?

EUGENE. If you're dead, what are you going to do with seven million dollars?

SELRIDGE. I told you. That's why I need ten days. I need a long weekend to spend the money. Give up, suckers, I got you all beat.

ARNOLD. Moronic. It's beyond moronic. It's sub-moronic.

SELRIDGE. Break their hearts, Jerome, and tell 'em my score.

EUGENE. It lacks poetry. I give Selridge a B.

SELRIDGE. (*angry*) A *B*? You give me a B? That creep signs a record contract that ain't worth shit and he gets a B? (*heads for money*) I want my money back.

WYKOWSKI. Touch that money and you're dead.

SELRIDGE. I was kidding. You think I was serious? I was kidding. (*He lies on his bunk.*) Who's next?

EUGENE. Hennesey.

HENNESEY. Me? I'm not ready yet.

EUGENE. It's your turn.

HENNESEY. I'm not good at things like this.

EUGENE. Come on. Just say it.

HENNESEY. I can't think of anything.

SELRIDGE. He can't think of anything. So he's out. Tough shit. Give him an F . . . Who's next?

HENNESEY. Okay. Okay . . . I'd spend it with my family.

WYKOWSKI. Is this guy serious?

CARNEY. Damn, I wish we were playing for big dough.

SELRIDGE. What an asshole.

HENNESEY. It's my last week. I can spend it any way I want. I'd like it to be with my family.

CARNEY. (*mimicking*) I'd like it to be with my family.

SELRIDGE. Go ahead, Jerome. What do you give him for *that* crap?

EUGENE. It's not interesting but at least it's honest . . . I give him a B-plus.

SELRIDGE. Okay. This game is fixed. I'm calling in the Military Police. I get a B for screwin' seven millionairesses and *he* gets a B-plus for goin' home to his mother? . . . I change my answer. I want to visit sick children in the hospital.

WYKOWSKI. Knock it off, Selridge. You had your turn.

EUGENE. It's yours now, Wykowski.

CARNEY. Don't let us down, Kowski. To some of us you're a hero.

WYKOWSKI. Okay . . . I always wanted to make it with a world-famous woman that nobody else could have. It didn't make no difference if she was beautiful or not, as long as I was the only one.

HENNESEY. Have you got someone in mind?

WYKOWSKI. (*smiles*) Yeah. I got someone in mind.

EUGENE. I think we're heading for an A-plus.

CARNEY. Who's the woman, Kowski?

WYKOWSKI. (*He does a grind and a bump.*) . . . The Queen of England! (*They all stare at him, dumbstruck.*)

CARNEY. The Queen of England????

SELRIDGE. That is disgusting. That's like making it with your grandmother.

EUGENE. Besides, you wouldn't be the only one. What about the *King* of England?

WYKOWSKI. Kings and Queens just do it once a year. To make a Prince. But I'd have her every day and every night for a week.

SELRIDGE. You couldn't get near her. They keep her under guard at Rockingham Palace.

WYKOWSKI. Not for me. She would say — (*high-pitched voice*) "Let that sexy Wykowski in my chamber."

ARNOLD. Apes and gorillas. I'm living with apes and gorillas.

HENNESEY. What's his score? Give him his score.

CARNEY. (*high-pitched English voice*) Yes. Give the Earl of Meatloaf his score.

EUGENE. This is a tough one. I find it completely un-redeeming in every way. Morally, ethically and sexually . . . but it's got style . . . *A*-minus!

SELRIDGE. (*furious*) Okay. I want my five bucks back. I'm not getting beat out by a guy who humps the Mother of the British Empire.

HENNESEY. Boy, I'm learning a lot about you guys to-night.

SELRIDGE. And versa visa, jerk-off.

WYKOWSKI. So I'm winning, right?

EUGENE. It's not over yet. There's two more to go.

SELRIDGE. Epstein's next. I want to hear what *his* last week on earth would be like. Probably wants to take an English exam at City College.

EUGENE. It's your turn, Arnold.

ARNOLD. There's no point to this game.

EUGENE. Yes, there is.

ARNOLD. What's the point?

EUGENE. I like it . . . Come on. It's your last week on earth. You're going to get killed overseas. What's your secret desire? (*They all look at EPSTEIN. . . . He thinks carefully.*)

ARNOLD. . . . I don't want to say. If I say it, it might not come true.

CARNEY. He doesn't have one. All he does is complain.

WYKOWSKI. And pass gas. That's his secret desire. He wants to bend over and blow up the world. (*SELRIDGE loves that one.*)

EUGENE. Wait a minute. Give him a chance. He has one . . . What is it, Arnold? What's the last thing you want to do on this earth? (*All attention is on EPSTEIN.*)

ARNOLD. . . . I would like to make Sergeant Merwin J. Toomey do two hundred push-ups in front of this platoon. (*There is stunned silence.*)

WYKOWSKI. That's good . . . I hate to admit it, but it's good.

SELRIDGE. It's okay. Five hundred would have been better.

EUGENE. I think it's terrific. I give Epstein an A-plus.

CARNEY. A-plus? You're crazy. Now you can't beat him.

EUGENE. I can still tie him.

WYKOWSKI. If it's a tie, all bets are off. Nobody wins.

EUGENE. Fair enough. Somebody else has to judge me. Pick a judge, Wykowski.

WYKOWSKI. (*smiles*) Sure, I pick Selridge.

SELRIDGE. I love it. No matter what crap he says, he gets an A-plus. Your money is safe, boys.

HENNESEY. Go on, Gene . . . Let's hear yours.

EUGENE. Okay. (*He takes a deep breath. They listen intently.*) . . . I'm going to get mine wiping out a whole battalion of Japanese marines. They'll put up a statue of me at Brighton Beach. Maybe name a junior high school after me, or a swimming pool. (*He poses.*)

SELRIDGE. All they'd give you is a locker room. The Eugene M. Jerome Locker Room.

HENNESEY. Let him finish. Go on, Gene.

EUGENE. Well . . . if it's my last week on earth . . . I would like to fall in love.

CARNEY. With who?

EUGENE. The perfect girl.

WYKOWSKI. There is no perfect girl.

EUGENE. If I fell in love with her, she'd be perfect.

WYKOWSKI. I told you. Jewish guys are all homos.

CARNEY. Incredible! . . . Okay, the game is over. Tell him what he got, Roy, and we'll all take our money back. (*They look at SELRIDGE.*)

WYKOWSKI. Go on. Tell him his score.

SELRIDGE. I give him a C-minus.

WYKOWSKI. What??

SELRIDGE. I'm sorry. I'm not gonna let him beat me with that pissy story. I came up with something "hot," I'm not gonna give him an A-plus for "Love in Bloom."

WYKOWSKI. Jesus, you are a moron. Go look in the latrine and see where you dropped your brains.

SELRIDGE. I couldn't help it. I couldn't.

EUGENE. You win, Arnold. It's your money. (*AR-NOLD starts for money.*)

WYKOWSKI. It never fails. It's always the Jews who end up with the money. Ain't that right, Roy?

SELRIDGE. Don't ask me. I never met a Jew before the army.

WYKOWSKI. They're easy to spot. (*to ARNOLD*) There's one . . . (*to EUGENE*) . . . And there's another one. (*to all*) They're the ones who slide the bacon under their toast so no one sees them eat it. Ain't that right, Jerome?

ARNOLD. (*calmly*) I'm tired of taking that Jew crap from you, Wykowski. I know you can probably beat the hell out of me, but I'm not going to take it from you anymore, understand?

WYKOWSKI. Sure you will. You'll take any shit from me . . . Come on. Come on. Let's see how tough you are. I'll knock the Alka-Seltzer right out of your asshole.

HENNESEY. Cut it out, Kowski. What difference does it make what religion he is?

WYKOWSKI. I didn't start it. Epstein's the one who thinks he's too good to take orders, isn't he? Well, I'm not doing a hundred push-ups for any God damn goof-up anymore. If he doesn't shape up, I'll bust his face whether he's got a Jew nose or not. (*They both go for each other, restrained by the others.*)

CARNEY. (*seeing TOOMEY off*) Ten-HUT!

(*Suddenly SERGEANT TOOMEY appears in his pants and an undershirt. All snap to attention.*)

TOOMEY. What the hell is going on here?

HENNESEY. Nothing, Sergeant.

TOOMEY. What do you mean nothing? I heard threats, challenges and an invitation to bust the nose of members of minority races. Now are you still telling me that nothing was going on here?

HENNESEY. Yes, Sergeant.

TOOMEY. I think you'd better sleep on that answer, boy. And to make sure you get a good night's sleep, you get yourself good and tired with one hundred push-ups. On the floor, dogface, and let me hear you count. (*HEN-NESEY gets on the ground and immediately starts to do push-ups.*) If I hear any more racial slurs from this platoon, some dumb bastard is going to be shoveling cow shit with a teaspoon for a month. Especially if I hear it from a Polack! LIGHTS OUT!

(*The lights suddenly go out leaving only a tiny spot on EUGENE.*)

EUGENE. (*to audience*) . . . I never liked Wykowski much and I didn't like him any better after tonight . . . But the one I hated most was myself because I didn't stand up for Epstein, a fellow Jew.

Maybe I was afraid of Wykowski or maybe it was because Epstein sort of sometimes asked for it, but since the guys didn't pick on me that much, I figured I'd just stay sort of neutral . . . like Switzerland . . .

Then I wrote in my memoirs what every guy's last desire would be if he was killed in the war.

I never intended to show it to anyone, but still I felt a little ashamed of betraying their secret and private thoughts . . . Possibly the only one who felt worse than I did was Hennesey on the floor.

HENNESEY. (*doing push-ups*) . . . 41 . . . 42 . . . 43 . . . 44 . . . 45.

(*Weeks later.*

A section of the latrine. SELRIDGE and CARNEY are finishing shaving. HENNESEY is brushing his hair. They are all in underwear, some with trousers on.)

SELRIDGE. Forty-eight hour pass, hot damn! If I make it with one woman every four hours, that means I could have . . . er . . . I could have . . . (*He thinks.*) — a lot of women!

HENNESEY. I'd be careful. You know what you could get.

SELRIDGE. Yeah. Relief.

WYKOWSKI. (*comes in, looking very angry*) Son of a bitch! God damn son of a bitch!!

SELRIDGE. What's wrong?

WYKOWSKI. (*holds up empty wallet*) Someone broke into my footlocker last night. They emptied my wallet. They took my pay and every cent I had in the world. Sixty-two bucks. Dirty bastard.

CARNEY. How do you know it was stolen? Maybe you lost it.

WYKOWSKI. I counted it before I hit the sack. I was saving it for the big weekend. Don't think I'm not wise to who did it. Maybe they both did it together.

HENNESEY. How do you know it was them? Maybe it was one of us.

WYKOWSKI. . . . Was it? Was it?

SELRIDGE. You think I'm crazy enough to tell you if I stole your money?

WYKOWSKI. It was Epstein, I'm telling you. He's trying to get back at me for what I said that night.

HENNESEY. Maybe he's sore at you but he's not the kind that steals money.

WYKOWSKI. Who asked you, Hennesey? What are you, one of those Irish Jews? All I did was call him a couple of names. Where I come from we're all Polacks, Dagos, Niggers and Sheenies. That stuff doesn't mean crap to me. You're a Mick, what do I care?

HENNESEY. Half Mick, half Nigger. (*WYKOWSKI and SELRIDGE look at each other.*)

WYKOWSKI. Are you serious?

HENNESEY. Yeah. My father's Irish, my mother's colored.

SELRIDGE. You can't be colored. They wouldn't let you in with us.

HENNESEY. I never told anybody.

WYKOWSKI. Yeah, but I guessed it. It was something I couldn't put my finger on but I knew something was wrong with you.

HENNESEY. I'm black Irish, that's as colored as I am. But now we know how you think, don't we, Kowski?

WYKOWSKI. I'm laying for you, Hennesey. After I get the bastard who stole my money, I'll settle my score with you.

CARNEY. Does Toomey know?

WYKOWSKI. I think so. He must have heard me. Somebody steals sixty-two bucks, people hear about it. (*TOOMEY appears.*)

TOOMEY. (*calmly*) Gentlemen, I think we have a problem. All those wishing to help me solve it, get your asses in here before the firing squad leaves for the weekend. ON THE DOUBLE!!! Ten-hut!!

(*The lights go up on the barracks area, off on latrine. All six soldiers rush in and line up at attention in front of their bunks. TOOMEY, dressed for weekend leave, walks slowly in front of them, thinking very seriously.*)

TOOMEY. (*continued*) . . . I've been in this man's army now for twelve years, four months and twenty-three days and during my tenure as a noncommissioned officer, I have put up with everything from mutiny to sodomy. I consider mutiny and sodomy relatively minor offenses. Mutiny is an act of aggression due to a rising expression of unreleased repressed feelings. Sodomy is the result of doing something you don't want to do with someone you don't want to do it with because of no access to do what you want to do with someone you can't get to do it with.

EUGENE. (*to audience*) It makes sense if you think it out slowly.

TOOMEY. Burglary, on the other hand, is a cheap shit crime. And I frown on that. In the past thirty-one days, you boys have made some fine progress. You're not fighting soldiers yet, but I'd match you up against some Nazi cocktail waitresses any time. That's why it was my recommendation that this platoon receive a forty-eight hour pass . . . But until we clear up the mystery of Private Wykowski's missing sixty-two dollars, there will be no forty-eight hour passes issued until you are old and gray soldiers of World War Two, marching as American Legionnaires in the Armistice Day Parade. I am asking the guilty party to place sixty-two dollars on this here footlocker within the next thirty seconds . . . I offer no leniency, no forgiveness and no abstention from punishment. What I do offer is honor and integrity, and the respect of his fellow soldiers, knowing that it was *his* act of courage that enabled them to enjoy the brief freedom they so richly deserve. (*He looks at his watch.*) I am counting down to thirty . . . It is of this time that heroes are made . . . One . . . two . . . three . . . four . . . five . . . (*They all look at each other silently.*) . . . six seven . . . eight . . .

(*Suddenly ARNOLD takes out his wallet, removes some bills, counts off sixty-two dollars and puts it on the footlocker in front of him. The others look silently ahead.*)

ARNOLD. There's sixty-two dollars, if anyone cares to count it.

TOOMEY. I don't think that will be necessary, Private Epstein . . . Wykowski, pick up your money. (*WYKOW-SKI picks it up and starts to count it.*) I SAID DON'T COUNT IT, BOY!!!! (*WYKOWSKI stops, folds it and puts it in his pocket and returns to attention.*) Private Epstein, do you have anything to say?

ARNOLD. No, Sergeant.

TOOMEY. May I ask why you decided to return the money?

ARNOLD. I chose to.

TOOMEY. You chose to. Knowing full well that swift and just punishment may be inflicted upon you when and if this is reported to the Commanding Officer?

ARNOLD. I know it only too well.

TOOMEY. You could have kept quiet about this incident. Chances are no one would have found out or been the wiser.

ARNOLD. I didn't see any reason why five innocent men should suffer a loss of privilege because of one guilty one.

TOOMEY. Private Wykowski . . . Is it your wish that I report this incident and the guilty party to the Commanding Officer?

WYKOWSKI. I just want my money, Sergeant. I can deal with the bastard who took it on my own. (*TOOMEY stares at him, then reaches into his pocket and takes out some folded bills.*)

TOOMEY. Last night at 0100 hours I wandered through this barracks and saw carelessness and complacency. Wykowski's wallet was lying in an open footlocker inviting weakness, avarice and temptation. *I* took your sixty-two dollars, Wykowski, and returned the empty wallet in its place. I did it to teach you a lesson . . . Instead, *I*

got . . . submarined. (*goes nose to nose with EPSTEIN*)
Private Epstein, are you such a God damn ignorant fool
to take the blame for something you were completely innocent of?

ARNOLD. The army has its logic, I have my own.

TOOMEY. The army's "logic" as you call it, is to instill
discipline, obedience and unquestioned faith in superi-
ors. What the hell is yours?

ARNOLD. Since I'm not guilty of a crime, I reserve the
privilege to keep my own motives a matter of confiden-
tiality.

TOOMEY. That's where you're wrong, soldier. Confessing to a crime you didn't commit is no less an offense to
not confessing to one you *did* commit. That is called
obstruction of justice. You may not like our rules, boy,
but by God, you're going to clean every toilet and piss-
pot until you learn them. Confined to barracks until
further notice. The rest of you are on forty-eight hours
leave. Fall out! . . . Epstein, I would like a word with
you in private. (*The others break up and move to their
bunks to discuss the event. ARNOLD follows TOOMEY
to the latrine. TOOMEY turns, faces EPSTEIN, lowers
his voice.*) Listen to me, you flyspeck on a mound of
horse shit. You're taking me on, ain't you? Well, you're
making a big mistake because I have a nutcracker that
crunches the testicles of men who take me on . . . How
the hell do you think you can beat me?

ARNOLD. I'm not trying to beat you, Sergeant. I'm
trying to work with you.

TOOMEY. (*looks at him sideways*) I think you're low
on batteries, Epstein. I think some plumber turned off
your fountain of knowledge. What the hell do you mean,
working with me?

ARNOLD. I don't think it's necessary to dehumanize a man to get him to perform. You can get better results raising our spirits than lowering our dignity.

TOOMEY. Why in the hell did you put back money you knew you didn't take?

ARNOLD. Because I knew that *you* did. I saw you take it. I think inventing a crime that didn't exist to enforce your theories of discipline is neanderthal in its conception.

TOOMEY. (*gets closer*) I can arrange it, Epstein, that from now on you get nothing to eat in the mess hall except cotton balls. You ever eat cotton balls, Epstein? You can chew it till 1986, it don't swallow . . . Men do not face enemy machine guns because they have been treated with kindness. They face them because they have a bayonet up their ass. I don't *want* them human. I want them obedient.

ARNOLD. Egyptian Kings made their slaves obedient. Eventually they lost their slaves *and* their kingdom.

TOOMEY. Yeah, well, I may lose mine but before you go, you're going to build me the biggest God damn pyramid you ever saw . . . I'm trying to save these boys' lives, you crawling bookworm. Stand in my way and I'll pulverize you into chicken droppings.

ARNOLD. It should be an interesting contest, Sergeant.

TOOMEY. After I crush your testicles, you can replace them with the cotton balls. (*He glares at ARNOLD, then exits quickly.*) . . . Neanderthal in its conception, Jesus Christ!

CARNEY. (*tying his tie*) So who really stole the money?

SELRIDGE. (*brushing his shoes*) Toomey stole Wykowski's sixty-two bucks but Epstein stole Toomey's *idea* of stealing Wykowski's sixty-two bucks.

HENNESEY. Why?

SELRIDGE. Did you ever see a big fat walrus screw another big fat walrus? There's no point to it but they do it anyway . . . You comin', Kows?

WYKOWSKI. In a minute.

CARNEY. I'll tell you something. The army is really dumb. If the navy is this dumb, we're gonna have to take a train to Europe. (*CARNEY and HENNESEY leave. ARNOLD returns to the room.*)

WYKOWSKI. I don't get you, Epstein. What'd you do a dumb-ass thing like that for?

ARNOLD. You wouldn't understand.

WYKOWSKI. Why not? Am I too dumb? Dumb Polack is that what I am? Now who's calling who names?

ARNOLD. You are. If no one confessed, no one goes on leave. If any of the other guys really did it, I'd end up cleaning the toilet bowls anyway. He's trying to break my spirit.

WYKOWSKI. How'd you figure that out?

ARNOLD. Talmudic reasoning.

WYKOWSKI. What?

ARNOLD. Talmudic. You weigh both sides of an issue, then choose the one that's the most interesting. Unless, of course, the other guy picks that one first.

WYKOWSKI. Yeah? Well, whatever . . . Anyway, I owe you one. You stuck your neck out for us. (*extends his hand*) I like to pay back my debts.

ARNOLD. (*looks at extended hand*) You really want to shake my hand, Wykowski?

WYKOWSKI. Listen, it's not going to come out again, so take your chance while you got it.

ARNOLD. Let's not be hypocritical. I did what I did for me, not for you.

WYKOWSKI. (*smiles*) I'm not going to make any more Jew cracks at you, Epstein. 'Cause you're a shitheel no matter what you are. (*He goes. The others go off, leaving EUGENE. EUGENE sits on his bed, smiles and shakes his head at ARNOLD.*)

EUGENE. Why do you always have to do things the hard way?

ARNOLD. It makes life more interesting.

EUGENE. It also makes a lot of problems.

ARNOLD. Without problems, the day would be over at eleven o'clock in the morning. (*ARNOLD starts to change into fatigues.*)

EUGENE. I admire what you did back there, Arnold. You remind me of my brother, sometimes. He was always standing up for his principles too.

ARNOLD. Principles are okay. But sometimes they get in the way of reason.

EUGENE. Then how do you know which one is the right one?

ARNOLD. You have to get involved. You don't get involved enough, Eugene.

EUGENE. What do you mean?

ARNOLD. You're a witness. You're always standing around *watching* what's happening. Scribbling in your book what other people do. You have to get in the middle of it. You have to take sides. Make a contribution to the fight.

EUGENE. What fight?

ARNOLD. *Any* fight. The one you believe in.

EUGENE. Yeah. I know what you mean. Sometimes I feel like I'm invisible. Like The Shadow. I can see everyone else but they can't see me. That's what I think writers are. Sort of invisible.

ARNOLD. Not Tolstoy. Not Dostoyevsky. Not Herman Melville.

EUGENE. Yeah. I have to read those guys.

TOOMEY. (*offstage*) EPSTEIN! I DON'T HEAR NO GOD DAMN FLUSHING!!

ARNOLD. I'd better go. I have to get involved with toilet bowls.

EUGENE. I'd love to talk to you more, Arnold.

ARNOLD. I'm available.

EUGENE. Well, maybe when I get back Sunday night.

ARNOLD. Sure. Anytime you want . . . Just make sure you don't come back pregnant.

EUGENE. Are you kidding? I'm wearing three pairs of socks.

ARNOLD. Make sure you put them on the right place. (*He leaves.*)

EUGENE. (*to audience*) Soo — I was off to Biloxi to live out my fantasies. Love or sex, I'd settle for either one . . . I put powder and Aqua Velva in and under every conceivable part of my body. (*CARNEY comes back in.*)

CARNEY. I've been waiting for you.

EUGENE. Okay. Let's go!

CARNEY. Wait — wait! I need a favor from you.

EUGENE. What is it?

CARNEY. Sit down. I need your opinion. And please, tell me the truth.

(*EUGENE waits, CARNEY lowers his head and begins to sing a romantic song of the period. After the first verse curtain starts to descend, as EUGENE looks helplessly at audience.*)

CURTAIN

ACT TWO

A section of a small, tacky room in a cheap hotel. There are two worn armchairs at angle to each other. Seated are EUGENE and CARNEY. SELRIDGE paces impatiently. All three are smoking cigarettes, puffing away nervously.

SELRIDGE. (*looks at his watch*) Almost a half hour he's been in there. It doesn't take a half hour. She couldn't make any money that way.

CARNEY. Maybe he went twice. Or three times.

SELRIDGE. Wykowski could keep going for six months straight. That's not the point. They charge you every time, that's the point.

CARNEY. Maybe she gave him a free one because of his unusual condition.

EUGENE. You mean she charges you every time you have a—?

SELRIDGE. (*pacing*) That's right.

EUGENE. How does she know when you have one?

SELRIDGE. (*stops, looks at him*) Because your eyes spin around and when they stop on two pineapples, you just had one. (*to CARNEY*) Is this guy for real?

CARNEY. And he's from New York City too. Can you believe it?

EUGENE. (*defensively*) I make out on my own. I just never go to places like this . . . And you mean, if you have a—a thing more than once, she keeps count?

CARNEY. Yeah. Actually, every time you do it, she makes an X on your head with her lipstick. (*He blows smoke in EUGENE's face.*)

EUGENE. Hey, don't blow smoke in my face. I'll stink up from tobacco.

CARNEY. Stop worrying. Nothing can penetrate your Aqua Velva . . . If you don't like it, what are you smoking for?

EUGENE. (*looks at cigarette in his hand*) I didn't know I was. Somebody must have handed it to me. (*He puts it out hard in the ashtray. He gets up and paces. To SELRIDGE:*) You want to sit down?

SELRIDGE. And break my concentration? (*looks at his watch*) Hurry up, dammit, I'm going to pass my peak.

EUGENE. What if she's ugly? I mean really ugly.

SELRIDGE. . . . Close your eyes and think of some girl in high school.

EUGENE. I don't want to close my eyes. That's the same as doing it to yourself.

SELRIDGE. Not if you're feeling somebody underneath you . . . Or on top of you.

EUGENE. (*stops*) What do you mean, on *top* of you. Who would be on top of me?

SELRIDGE. She would. She could be anywhere. Under a table. On a chair or an ironing board.

EUGENE. *An ironing board???* What kind of girl is this? I thought we were going just to a regular place.

SELRIDGE. I didn't mention anything that wasn't regular. I mean don't you know anything? Do you have any idea of how many possible positions there are?

EUGENE. Yeah. Sure. I'm not an ignoramus.

CARNEY. (*to EUGENE*) How many positions are there?

EUGENE. (*looks at CARNEY, points to SELRIDGE*) I'm having this conversation with him.

SELRIDGE. Okay. How many positions are there?

EUGENE. (*thinks*) . . . American or Worldwide?

SELRIDGE. (*laughs*) You don't know shit, Jerome.

EUGENE. Maybe not actual experience. But I have all the information I need.

SELRIDGE. Then how many positions are there, in this galaxy?

EUGENE. For how much?

SELRIDGE. Loser pays for the bang.

EUGENE. Don't call it a bang. I'm here for pleasure, not to get banged.

CARNEY. (*laughs*) This guy's a riot.

SELRIDGE. For five bucks. How many positions are there?

EUGENE. I'm thinking. Give me a minute.

SELRIDGE. You want me to tell you?

EUGENE. No.

SELRIDGE. Well, I'll tell you. Seventeen.

EUGENE. How do you know?

SELRIDGE. Because I've tried them all.

EUGENE. You're wrong. There's at least *52* different positions.

SELRIDGE. *52??* . . . You're crazy! . . . Where'd you get that from?

EUGENE. I saw a dirty deck of cards once.

SELRIDGE. (*to CARNEY*) This guy's worse than Epstein.

EUGENE. You owe me five bucks.

SELRIDGE. Listen, twirp. You're lucky if you do *one* position.

EUGENE. I'm not going to do *anything* if it's on an ironing board.

CARNEY. Why not? You'll get your shirt pressed for free. (*SELRIDGE looks at his watch.*)

SELRIDGE. Thirty-four minutes. Damn Wykowski! We should have let the normal guys go first.

(*EUGENE crosses down and addresses the audience.*)

EUGENE. (*to audience*) . . . I didn't want my first time to be like this . . . I really tried to meet somebody nice but there are twenty-one thousand soldiers on leave in Biloxi and fourteen girls . . . Those are tough odds . . . Especially since the fourteen girls all go to Catholic school and are handcuffed to Nuns . . .

(*WYKOWSKI appears with a know-it-all look on his face. He straightens his tie as he chews gum.*)

SELRIDGE. Well??? . . . Tell us!
WYKOWSKI. . . . She wants to see me again after the war. (*He puts on his cap and disappears.*)
SELRIDGE. (*looks around*) Okay, whose turn is it?
EUGENE. You go ahead. I just had lunch. I don't want to get cramps. (*CARNEY nods assent.*)
SELRIDGE. (*straightens self up*) I'll try to leave a little something for you guys. (*He disappears.*) Hey! How are you?
CARNEY. (*looks at EUGENE*) We don't have to do this, you know. There's a dance over at the U.S.O.
EUGENE. This isn't your first time, is it? I mean, you've done it before, haven't you?
CARNEY. Oh, yeah. Sure. Are you kidding? . . . Not a lot. About five or six times.
EUGENE. So why are you doing it again?
CARNEY. You're not through after five or six times. If

you live long enough, you've got twelve thousand more left.

EUGENE. I don't know why I'm so scared. I'm never going to see her again. I just don't want to seem foolish. I think I'm afraid she's going to laugh at me.

CARNEY. Not if she gets paid. If she laughed at you, you would be entitled to a refund. (*SELRIDGE comes out, buttoning his shirt.*)

EUGENE. You're through already? That was fast.

SELRIDGE. (*He snaps his fingers.*) I didn't make it to the bed. I knew I hit my peak too soon. (*And he is gone.*)

CARNEY. (*looks at EUGENE*) Listen, I think I'm gonna go to the dance.

EUGENE. How come?

CARNEY. I said before I did it five or six times but it was all with the same girl. We're sort of engaged. She might not like it.

EUGENE. I bet she wouldn't. I didn't know you had a girl. That's terrific. What's her name?

CARNEY. Charlene.

EUGENE. Charlene! Wow! Sounds sexy. You think you'll get married?

CARNEY. Well, it's a fifty-fifty chance. She's got another boyfriend in Albany . . . So what are you going to do?

EUGENE. Well, the thing is, I don't have a girl. I've got to learn on my own. Epstein says I have to get more involved in life. I think I'm in the perfect place for an involvement.

CARNEY. Okay. Maybe I'll see you later. (*He puts on his cap.*) Listen. Don't expect too much the first time. What I mean is, if it doesn't go all that terrific, don't give up on it for good.

EUGENE. I'm not a quitter. I'm dedicating my life to getting it right.

CARNEY. You putting this in your memoirs?

EUGENE. Sure. I put everything in my memoirs.

CARNEY. That's smart. Because people don't like books unless there's sex in it . . . Good luck, kid. (*He takes a photo of EUGENE with his hand on the door.*)

EUGENE. (*to audience*) . . . And thus, the young man they called Eugene, bade farewell to his youth, turned and entered the Temple of Fire.

(*Scenery changes to ROWENA's room. EUGENE hidden behind a screen, ROWENA sitting at her vanity, smoking, trying to be patient.*)

ROWENA. (*calls out*) How you doing, honey?

EUGENE. (*behind screen*) Okay.

ROWENA. You having any trouble in there?

EUGENE. No. No trouble.

ROWENA. What the hell you doing for ten minutes? C'mon, kid. I haven't got all day. (*EUGENE appears. He is wearing his khaki shorts, shoes and socks. A cigarette dangles from his lips. ROWENA looks at him.*) Listen. You can keep your shorts on if you want but I have a rule against wearing army shoes in bed.

EUGENE. (*looks down*) Oh. I'm sorry. I just forgot to take them off. (*He sits on the bed and very slowly starts to unlace them. To audience:*) I started to sweat like crazy. I prayed my Aqua Velva was working. (*ROWENA sprays around her with perfume from atomizer.*)

ROWENA. You don't mind a little perfume, do you, honey? The boy before you had on a gallon of Aqua Velva.

EUGENE. (*looks at audience then at her*) No, I don't mind. You can spray some on me. (*She smiles and sprays him playfully.*) Gee, it smells good.

ROWENA. If you'd like a bottle for your girl friend, I sell them. Five dollars apiece.

EUGENE. You sell perfume too?

ROWENA. I sell hard to get items. Silk stockings. Black panties . . . You interested?

EUGENE. (*earnestly*) . . . Do you carry men's clothing?

ROWENA. (*laughs*) That's cute. You're cute, honey . . . You want me to take your shoes off?

EUGENE. I can do it. Honest. I can do it. (*He gets his first shoe off.*)

ROWENA. Is this your first time?

EUGENE. My first time? (*He laughs.*) Are you kidding? That's funny . . . Noo . . . It's my second time . . . The first time they were closed.

ROWENA. You don't smoke cigarettes either, do you? (*She takes cigarette out of EUGENE's mouth.*)

EUGENE. How'd you know?

ROWENA. You looked like your face was on fire . . . If you want to look older, why don't you try a mustache?

EUGENE. I did but it wouldn't grow in on the left side . . . What's your name?

ROWENA. Rowena . . . What's yours?

EUGENE. My name? (*to audience*) I suddenly panicked. Supposing this girl kept a diary.

ROWENA. Well?

EUGENE. (*quickly*) Jack . . . Er . . . Jack Mulgroovey.

ROWENA. Yeah? I knew a *Tom* Mulgreevy once.

EUGENE. No. Mine is Mulgroovey. Oo not ee.

ROWENA. Where you from, Jack?

EUGENE. (*slight accent*) Texarkana.

ROWENA. Is that right?

EUGENE. Yes, ma'am.

ROWENA. Is that Texas or Arkansas?

EUGENE. Arkansas, I think.

ROWENA. You *think*?

EUGENE. I left there when I was two. Then we moved to Georgia.

ROWENA. Really? You a cracker?

EUGENE. What's a cracker?

ROWENA. Someone from Georgia.

EUGENE. Oh, yeah. I'm a cracker. The whole family's crackers . . . Were you born in Biloxi?

ROWENA. No. Gulfport. I still live there with my husband.

EUGENE. Your husband?? . . . You're married?? . . . My God! If he finds me here he'll kill me.

ROWENA. No he won't.

EUGENE. Does he know that you're a—you're a—

ROWENA. Sure he does. That's how we met. He's in the navy. He was one of my best customers. He still is.

EUGENE. You mean you *charge* your own husband??

ROWENA. I mean he's my best lover . . . You gonna do it from there, cowboy? 'Cause I'll have to make some adjustments.

EUGENE. I'm ready. (*to ROWENA*) Here I come. (*She holds open blanket. He gets into the bed and clings to the side.*)

ROWENA. If you're gonna hang on the edge like that, we're gonna be on the floor in two minutes.

EUGENE. I didn't want to crowd you.

ROWENA. Crowding is what this is all about, Tex. (*She pulls him over. He kneels above her.*) Okay, honey. Do your stuff.

EUGENE. What stuff is that?

ROWENA. Whatever you like to do.

EUGENE. Why don't you start and I'll catch up.

ROWENA. Didn't anyone ever tell you what to do?

EUGENE. My brother once showed me but you look a lot different than my brother.

ROWENA. You're sweet. I went to high school with a boy like you. I had the biggest damn crush on him.

EUGENE. (*still above her*) Do you have a hanky?

ROWENA. Anything wrong?

EUGENE. My nose is running. (*She takes hanky, wipes his nose.*)

ROWENA. Better?

EUGENE. Thank you. Listen, please don't be offended but I really don't care if this is a wonderful experience or not. I just want to get it over with.

ROWENA. Whatever you say . . . Lights on or off?

EUGENE. Actually I'd like a blindfold. (*She reaches over and turns off lamp.*) . . . Oh, God . . . Oh, MY GOD!!! (*slumps down*) . . . WOW! . . . I DID IT! . . . I DID IT!!

ROWENA. Anything else, honey?

EUGENE. (*calmer, more mature*) Yes. I'd like two bottles of perfume and a pair of black panties.

(*Blackout.*

Lights up on section of barracks. It's late Sunday night. SELRIDGE, CARNEY and ARNOLD are lying on their bunks. WYKOWSKI, pacing, has EUGENE's notebook of memoirs. CARNEY is on his stomach reading a letter and ARNOLD is reading a worn paperback of Kafka.)

WYKOWSKI. . . . I can't believe what this creep's been writing about us . . . Listen to this . . . "No matter how lunatic I think Sergeant Toomey is, there is method to his madness. He is winning the game. Each day we drop a little of our own personalities and become more obedient, more robot-like, until what was once an intelligent, thinking human being is now nothing but a khaki idiot. Yesterday, in front of everybody, he made Epstein unscrew the top of his head and take his brains out."

ARNOLD. (*without looking up from his book*) I fooled him. I only took out my mucous membranes.

WYKOWSKI. (*continues reading*) . . . "I am fighting hard to retain my identity, and the only time I am able to hold on to who I am is in the still, still of the night."

(*HENNESEY comes in from outside.*)

HENNESEY. Wow, what a weekend. How'd you guys do?

WYKOWSKI. Hey, Hennesey. You ought to listen to this. You're in this too.

HENNESEY. What is it? (*He starts loosening tie.*)

WYKOWSKI. *The Secret and Private Memoirs of Eugene M. Jerome.*

HENNESEY. He let you read it?

WYKOWSKI. No, but we're going to ask him if it's alright when we get through. (*He and SELRIDGE laugh.*)

HENNESEY. You have no right to read that. That's like opening someone's mail.

WYKOWSKI. Bullshit. It's all about us. Private things about every one of us. That's public domain like in the newspapers.

ARNOLD. (*without looking up from his book*) A newspaper is published. Unpublished memoirs are the sole and private property of the writer.

WYKOWSKI. I thought all Jews were doctors. I didn't know they were lawyers too.

ARNOLD. I'm not a Jew anymore, Wykowski.

WYKOWSKI. What do you mean?

ARNOLD. I converted to Catholicism yesterday. In six weeks I hope to become a priest and my first act of service to the Holy Father is to have you excommunicated, so get off my ass.

SELRIDGE. (*laughs*) That's good. That's funny. God damn Jews are really funny. Hey, Epstein, I'm beginning to like you, I swear to Christ.

WYKOWSKI. (*annoyed*) You guys interested in hearing the rest of this or not?

HENNESEY. No, I'm not. (*He starts toward latrine, stops.*) I thought you were Gene's friend, Epstein.

ARNOLD. He didn't lock his locker. Why then would he leave something so private in an open locker? There's no logic to it. I have no interest in illogical things.

HENNESEY. (*to EPSTEIN*) You tell Gene I had nothing to do with this. You hear me? (*He exits to latrine.*)

SELRIDGE. Go on. After ". . . still, still of the night."

WYKOWSKI. (*reads*) . . . "At night I listen to the others breathing in their sleep and it's then that their fears and self-doubts become even more apparent than during their waking hours . . . One night a sudden scream from Selridge that sounded like he was calling out the name, Louise. Is Louise his girl or possibly his mother?"

SELRIDGE. He's full of crap.

WYKOWSKI. Who's Louise?

SELRIDGE. My mother. But he's full of crap. I never called my mother Louise.

WYKOWSKI. Poor baby, wants his mother. (*continues reading*)

CARNEY. I don't want to hear any more of this. I don't like being spied on.

WYKOWSKI. (*looks at book*) Dirty bastard! Wait'll

you hear what he writes about me. (*Suddenly EUGENE appears, coming back from town.*)

SELRIDGE. It's him. Put it away.

(*WYKOWSKI slips the book under his bunk, pretends to play cards with SELRIDGE. EUGENE enters with a big, self-satisfied smile on his face and a very "cocky" walk.*)

EUGENE. Hi, guys! (*They all look up, mutter their hellos and resume their activities. EUGENE waits expectantly for someone to ask about his adventure but no one does.*) So how was your weekend?

CARNEY. Fine

WYKOWSKI. Great.

SELRIDGE. The best.

EUGENE. Good—good—good—good—good.

CARNEY. (*to EUGENE*) Well?

EUGENE. Well what?

CARNEY. What was it like? Give us details . . . Was it "Empty Saddles in the Old Corral" or was it "Swing Swing Swing"?

EUGENE. It was sort of—"Moonlight Cocktails" . . . It was chatty.

WYKOWSKI. Chatty?? Your first time in the sack with a pro was "chatty"?

EUGENE. She's not a pro. She only does it on weekends.

WYKOWSKI. So what does that make her? A semi-pro?

SELRIDGE. (*laughs*) Great! That was great. Perfect remark, Kows . . .

EUGENE. At least we talked to each other. I wasn't in and out of there in two seconds. She was a person to me, not a pro.

EPSTEIN. (*still reading book*) Self-righteous, Eugene.

Be on guard against self-righteousness.

EUGENE. (*He unties his tie, starts to unbutton his shirt.*) . . . The second time was "Swing Swing Swing." (*He smiles.*)

SELRIDGE. The *second* time? You paid twice?

EUGENE. No. It was a "freebie." On the house.

WYKOWSKI. You're full of it.

CARNEY. Why would she give you a free one?

EUGENE. Maybe I was her one millionth customer. (*He chuckles at his joke.*)

WYKOWSKI. Hey, Jerome. Blow it out your barracks bag. (*EUGENE doesn't see what he's looking for. He seems disturbed. He looks through locker, under his bunk and mattress.*)

EUGENE. Has anyone seen my notebook?

WYKOWSKI. (*very deliberate*) What notebook is that?

EUGENE. The one I'm always writing in . . . Arnold, did you see it?

ARNOLD. Why did you leave your locker unlocked?

EUGENE. Because I lost my key in the shower drain. There was nothing valuable in there except my book. I thought I could trust people around here.

WYKOWSKI. That's really funny, Jerome, 'cause we thought we could trust you too.

EUGENE. What does that mean? (*WYKOWSKI reaches under his bunk and takes out the notebook. He opens it up and EUGENE makes a move toward it but WYKOWSKI jumps on top of his bunk and extends his foot to ward off EUGENE. He starts to read.*)

WYKOWSKI. "One night a sudden scream from Selridge that sounded like he was calling out the name Louise. Is Louise his girl or possibly his mother?"

EUGENE. (*furious*) You had no right to read that. Give it to me, Kowski.

CARNEY. Give it to him. Nobody's interested.

WYKOWSKI. No? You interested in what he thinks about you, Donny baby?

EUGENE. (*lunges for him*) Give it to me, Goddammit!! (*SELRIDGE reaches quickly and grabs EUGENE's arm and bends it behind his back. EUGENE knows one move and it's broken.*)

SELRIDGE. I'm just gonna hold your arm. If you want it broken, it's up to you.

CARNEY. What does he say about me?

EUGENE. Kowski, please don't read it.

WYKOWSKI. If it gets boring, I'll stop. (*He reads.*) "I can't make Don Carney out yet. Basically I like him and we've had some interesting talks, if you don't mind sticking to popular music and baseball. But there's something about him you can't count on and if I was ever in real trouble, Don Carney's the last one I'd turn to." (*CARNEY and EUGENE look at each other. The others are quiet.*)

CARNEY. Well, let's just hope you never have to count on me. (*He is hurt. He gets up, walks to the side and lights up a cigarette.*)

EUGENE. (*to CARNEY*) It doesn't mean anything. It's just the thoughts in my head when I'm writing it. They change every day.

HENNESEY. Let him go, Selridge.

SELRIDGE. You want to take his place? I don't care whose arm I break.

WYKOWSKI. Okay, you ready for the best part? Here's the best part . . . (*He reads.*) "Wykowski is pure animal. His basic instincts are all physical and he eats his meals like a horse eating his oats." Hey, Epstein! Can I sue him for defamation of—what is it?

ARNOLD. Character. Only if his intent is to prove malice and in your case it's not possible.

SELRIDGE. Go on. What else does he say about you?

WYKOWSKI. (*reads on*) "He masturbates in bed four or five times a night. He has no shame about it and his capacities are inexhaustible. Sometimes when he has a discharge, he announces it to the room. "Number five torpedo fired! Loading number six!" (*to others*) That's really good reporting. This guy should be on *Time* Magazine or something.

EUGENE. (*near tears*) Please stop it. You want to read it, read it to yourself.

WYKOWSKI. What do you mean? You're making me famous. Maybe the movies'll buy this. Great picture for John Wayne.

SELRIDGE. Is there any more?

WYKOWSKI. Yeah. Where was I?

SELRIDGE. You just fired number five.

WYKOWSKI. Oh yeah. Here. (*He reads.*) "Despite Wykowski's lack of culture, sensitivity or the pursuit of anything minutely intellectual, his greatest strength is his consistency of character and his earnest belief that he belongs on the battlefield. He is clearly the best soldier in the platoon, dependable under pressure and it would not surprise me if Wykowski came out of this war with the Medal of Honor." (*WYKOWSKI looks at EUGENE.*) . . . You really mean that, Jerome?

EUGENE. I told you, I don't mean any of it. I get a thought and I write it down. Right now I would describe you in three words. "A yellow bastard!"

WYKOWSKI. They don't give the Medal of Honor to yellow bastards . . . Let him go, Sel. (*SELRIDGE lets him go, EUGENE rubs his arm in pain.*) . . . Why do you want to write this stuff down for? You're just gonna make a lot of guys unhappy.

EUGENE. What I write is *my* business. Give me my book. (*He reaches for it.*)

ARNOLD. Wait a minute. (*As WYKOWSKI extends book, ARNOLD snatches it from his hand.*) I think I deserve to hear *my* life story.

EUGENE. Arnold, I beg you. Don't read it. They're my private thoughts and if you take them, you steal from me.

ARNOLD. I gather then it's unflattering. Don't you know me by now, Gene? I can't be unflattered. I'm past it . . . However, if you don't want me to read it, I won't read it. But I don't think we'll be able to be truly honest with each other from this moment on.

EUGENE. (*looks at him*) . . . Put it back when you're through. (*He gets up and walks out of the room. AR-NOLD opens the book and starts to read to himself.*)

WYKOWSKI. Don't we get to hear it?

ARNOLD. Sure, Kowski. This is what we're fighting the war about, isn't it? (*He reads.*) "Arnold Epstein is truly the most complex and fascinating man I've ever met and his constant and relentless pursuit of truth, logic and reason fascinates me in the same proportion as his obstinacy and unnecessary heroics drive me to distraction. But I love him for it. In the same manner that I love Joe DiMaggio for making the gesture of catching a long fly ball to center seem like the last miracle performed by God in modern times. But often I hold back showing my love and affection for Arnold because I think he might misinterpret it. It just happens to be my instinctive feeling — that Arnold is homosexual, and it bothers me that it bothers me." (*He closes the book. He looks at the others who are all staring at him.*) . . . Do you see why I find life so interesting? Here is a man of my own faith and background, potentially intelligent and talented, who in six weeks has come to the brilliant conclusion that a cretin like Wykowski is going to win the Medal of Honor and that I, his most esteemed and dearest friend, is a fairy. (*He tosses the book on EUGENE's bunk.*) This is a problem worthy of a Talmudic scholar. Goodnight, fellas . . . It is my opinion that no one gets a wink of sleep tonight.

(*Light up on the steps outside the barracks. A bare light bulb hangs above. EUGENE sits on the steps, smoking a cigarette and looking in the depths of despair. After a few moments, DON CARNEY comes out, leans against the post and lights up a cigarette.*)

CARNEY. . . . Did she really give you a second one for free? (*There is a moment's silence.*)

EUGENE. Listen, I'm sorry about what I wrote in the book. I didn't mean it the way it sounded.

CARNEY. Forget about it. You don't really know me anyway.

EUGENE. No. I suppose I don't.

CARNEY. . . . Is that what you think? That I'm someone who can't be counted on?

EUGENE. I don't know. You're just somebody who can never make up his mind. You say, "Let's go eat Chinese food." We walk in and order and then you say, "No, let's go get some burgers" . . . We play basketball and you never take a shot. You always pass off to somebody.

CARNEY. Because I'm not a good shooter.

EUGENE. You're as good as the rest of us. You just think about it too long. Then it's too late to take the shot . . .

CARNEY. And that's why I can't be counted on?

EUGENE. I wasn't writing about peacetime. I'm sure you're very dependable in peacetime. But we're at war. We're going to be fighting for our lives soon. I mean, somebody throws a grenade into your foxhole, you don't want some guy staring at it for ten minutes saying, "What do you think we ought to do about it?"

CARNEY. Yeah, I can see that.

EUGENE. But you're still sore at me, aren't you?

CARNEY. I don't know. I have to think about it.

EUGENE. I figured you did.

CARNEY. . . . You know what Charlene once said to me? She said the reason she was seeing this other guy in Albany was because she didn't think I was someone she could count on.

EUGENE. You're kidding? Those exact words?

CARNEY. You think I'd ever forget them? She said she really liked me more than him but she wasn't sure I'd ever make up my mind. She didn't want to wait for me forever. So while she's waiting, she sees this guy up in Albany.

EUGENE. You see? That's what I meant.

CARNEY. Except for one thing. I'm not going to be in a foxhole with her with some Jap throwing in a grenade. I *have* to think about this because getting married is more serious.

EUGENE. More serious than being blown up?

CARNEY. Sure. Because if the grenade goes off, it's all over. Two seconds and you're gone. But if you make a mistake in marriage, you've got fifty years of misery. See what I mean?

EUGENE. Yeah. I see. (*He gets up, yawns.*) Well, I'm tired. I'm going to turn in. How about you?

CARNEY. I don't know. Maybe.

(*EUGENE looks at the audience and nods as if to say,* "Didn't I tell you?" *He starts off.*)

EUGENE. G'night.

CARNEY. G'night.

(*EUGENE goes inside. CARNEY sings a sentimental song of the period. The others wake up, angry. CARNEY retreats, lies down.*
The barracks. Moonlight coming in through the window. Suddenly the lights switch on. All six men are in their underwear, in their bunks. TOOMEY bangs loudly on the bed with his clipboard.)

TOOMEY. UP! Everybody UP!! Goddammit!!! it is two-fifteen in the morning and I've got a headache, a problem and a God damn temper all at the same time. Move your asses, we've got some serious talking to do. MOVE IT! (*He bangs bedpost again. They all get out of bed, mumbling their surprise and indignation. All stand at attention beside their bunks. TOOMEY paces back and forth, silently and angrily.*) . . . Is there any among you who does not know the meaning of the word, fellatio? (*Some of them look at each other.*) For the uninformed, fellatio is the act of committing oral intercourse . . . Is there any among you who does not know the meaning of the word "oral" or "intercourse"? . . . It is encouraging to know that my platoon is made up of mental giants . . .
At exactly 0155 this morning, Sergeant Riley of Baker Company entered the darkened latrine situated in his barracks . . . When he hit the light switch, lo and behold, he encountered two members of this regiment in the act of the aforementioned exercise . . . When I was in the Boy Scouts, that kind of thing came under the heading of "experimentation" . . . In the wartime U.S. Army, it is considered a criminal offense, punishable by court-martial, dishonorable discharge and a possible five year prison term . . . The soldier in Company B was a—

(*looks at clipboard*) — Private Harvey J. Lindstrom. The other soldier, whose back was to Sergeant Riley, was not seen and made his escape by jumping out an open window with his pants somewhere around his ankles, a feat of dexterity worthy of a paratrooper . . . Sergeant Riley, a man with five pounds of shrapnel in his right leg, gave chase to no avail but reported seeing the man enter this barracks at approximately oh two hundred hours . . . These are the facts, gentlemen. I will be brief. Does the guilty party wish to step forward, admit his indiscretion and save this company, what I promise you, will be pain, anguish and humiliation beyond the endurance of man? (*No one moves.*) No, I didn't think so . . . I'm just going to have to pick him out, won't I? . . . It's amazing what you can find out when you go eyeball to eyeball . . . (*He crosses to WYKOWSKI and indeed goes eyeball to eyeball. He moves on and does it with all six men.*) Don't blink, Selridge . . . Look at me . . . Stand up, soldier . . . (*No one breathes. No one bats an eye.*) . . . There were two eyeballs in there whose shoes I wouldn't want to be in . . . Private Lindstrom will be interrogated in the morning. If he names the man he consorted with tonight, it is very possible Private Lindstrom's sentence will be significantly lessened. A worrisome thought to the gentleman whose eyeballs I just referred to . . . In the meantime all privileges on base are cancelled, all weekend leaves are likewise cancelled . . . The moral of this story is — when you get real horny, do unto yourself what you would otherwise do unto others . . . (*He turns and leaves. The others breathe at last and finally look at each other.*)

WYKOWSKI. . . . . Okay, what are we going to do about this?

EUGENE. Don't say it, Wykowski. Just don't say it.

WYKOWSKI. I don't have to say it. We all know who he's talking about. We all know who it is. You even wrote it down in your book, didn't you? . . . Well, didn't you?

EUGENE. I also wrote down you're an animal. If I'm right then you should be in the cavalry with a saddle on your back. I'll show it to Toomey, okay? Then Epstein can start serving his five years and you can move into the stables. That should satisfy a horse's ass like you.

CARNEY. Cut it out! Both of you! It's none of our business. Let the Army take care of it.

SELRIDGE. No more base privileges? No more weekend passes? You're telling me that's not my business.

HENNESEY. Carney's right. The Army'll take care of it.

EUGENE. (*to ARNOLD*) I'm sorry, Arnold. I swear to God, I'm sorry I ever wrote it.

ARNOLD. (*cheerfully*) Actually I'm rather enjoying it. It's like an Agatha Christie story. *Murder by Fellatio*. Title's no good. Sounds like Italian ice cream . . . How about *Murder on the Fellatio Express*?

WYKOWSKI. You think this is funny, Epstein? Let's see if you'll be laughing at Leavenworth . . . And he calls *me* a cretin.

HENNESEY. There's nothing we can do about it tonight. Why don't we hit the sack. (*He gets into his bunk.*)

SELRIDGE. (*getting into his bunk*) I don't see what's such a big deal. A guy should be able to do what he wants to do . . . Just as long as he doesn't do it to me. (*He glares at EPSTEIN. EUGENE takes a page from his memoirs, tears it out and rips it up.*)

ARNOLD. That's a mistake, Gene . . . Once you start compromising your thoughts, you're a candidate for mediocrity.

(*They all get into their bunks. The lights go out except a pin spot on EUGENE who sits up and looks at audience.*)

EUGENE. . . . I learned a very important lesson that night. People believe whatever they read. Something magical happens once it's put down on paper. They figure no one would go to the trouble of writing it down if it wasn't the truth. Responsibility was my new watchword. (*We hear a phone ring once.*) Anyway, the army must have really scared Private Harvey J. Lindstrom that night because I knew when I heard the phone ring in Sergeant Toomey's room, the poor guy must have talked his guts out. I went out for a smoke because what happened in the next ten seconds was something I didn't want to see or hear.

(*The lights in the barracks go on and SERGEANT TOOMEY stands there in his pants, his shirt unbuttoned and strapping a Sam Browne belt which holds a pistol in a holster. He stands there a moment. He is not happy about the task he is about to perform. The others sit up and look at him.*)

TOOMEY. When the following soldier's name is called, he is requested to dress in his class A uniform . . . and follow me . . . Hennesey, James J.! (*The others look surprised and turn towards HENNESEY.*)
HENNESEY. . . . What for?
TOOMEY. That's a matter you can discuss with the military police . . . Come on, son. I don't like this any better than you do.

(*HENNESEY looks at the others for help. There is none
    forthcoming. He gets up and slips into his pants. He
    puts on his shirt and begins to button it. He steps
    down front away from the group, putting his tie on.
    He suddenly begins to sob.*
Lights out on the barracks.
Light up on EUGENE in limbo.)

EUGENE. (*to audience*) . . . I felt real lousy about Hennesey . . . The next weekend I went to Rowena's again . . .
She didn't even remember me . . . She acted like I was a
stranger . . . I tell her about Hennesey doing it with another guy and maybe getting five years in jail and she
says, "Well, I haven't got too much sympathy for their
kind, sweetheart. They're just taking the bread out of the
mouths of my babies" . . . I'm never going to pay for it
again . . . It just cheapens the whole idea of sex . . . (*The
sets begin to change into the U.S.O.*) . . . I was determined
to meet the perfect girl. I knew just what she would be
like . . . She's going to be pretty but not too beautiful.
When they're too beautiful, they love them first and you
second . . . And she'll be athletic. Someone I could hit
fly balls to and she'd catch all of them. She'll love to
go to the movies and read books and see plays and we'd
never run out of conversation . . . She's out there, I know
it. Right now the girl I'm going to fall in love with is living in New York or Boston or Philadelphia—walking
around the streets, not even knowing I'm alive. It's crazy.
(*Light up on U.S.O. DAISY dancing with a soldier.*)
—There she is and here I am. The both of us just waiting
around to meet. Why doesn't she just yell out, "Eugene!
I'm here! Come and get me" . . . (*The dance ends. Soldier goes off. DAISY crosses to EUGENE.*)

DAISY. Hello.

EUGENE. (*turns*) Hi. (*He looks to audience then back
to DAISY.*)

DAISY. Would you care to dance?

EUGENE. Me? Oh. Well, I don't dance very well.

DAISY. I bet you do.

EUGENE. No. I swear. I never dance.

DAISY. Then why did you come to a dance?

EUGENE. That's a logical question. Because I like to talk. And I was hoping I'd meet someone I felt like talking to.

DAISY. We could talk while we dance.

EUGENE. It's hard for me because I'm always counting when I dance. Whatever you said, I would answer, "one two, one two."

DAISY. (*laughs*) Well, I'll only ask you mathematical questions. (*EUGENE laughs as well.*) I'll bet you didn't know how to march before you got into the army.

EUGENE. No, I didn't.

DAISY. Well, if you could learn to march, you can learn to dance.

EUGENE. Yeah, except if I didn't learn to march, I'd be doing push-ups till I was eighty-three.

DAISY. I'm not that strict. But if it makes you that uncomfortable I won't intrude on your privacy. It was very nice meeting you. Goodbye. (*She starts to walk away. She gets a few steps when EUGENE calls out.*)

EUGENE. Okay!

DAISY. Okay what?

EUGENE. One two, one two.

DAISY. Are you sure?

EUGENE. Positive.

DAISY. Good. (*She crosses to him, then stands in front of him and raises her left arm up and right arm in position to hold his wrist.*)

EUGENE. All I have to do is step into place, right?

DAISY. Right. (*He tucks his cap in his belt and then steps into place, taking her hand and her waist and he starts to dance. It's not Fred Astaire but it's not too awkward.*) You're doing fine. Except your lips are moving.

EUGENE. If my lips don't move, my feet don't move.

DAISY. Well, try talking instead of counting.

EUGENE. Okay . . . Let's see . . . My name is Gene. (*softly*) One two, one two . . . Sorry.

DAISY. It's okay. We're making headway. Just plain Gene?

EUGENE. If you want the long version, it's Eugene Morris Jerome. What's yours?

DAISY. Daisy!

EUGENE. Daisy? That's funny because Daisy's my favorite character in literature.

DAISY. Daisy Miller or Daisy Buchanan?

EUGENE. Buchanan. *The Great Gatsby* is one of the all-time great books. Actually I never read *Daisy Miller.* Is it good?

DAISY. It's wonderful. Although I preferred *The Great Gatsby.* New York must have been thrilling in the twenties.

EUGENE. It was, it was . . . That's where I'm from . . . Well, I only saw a little of it from my baby carriage, but it's still a terrific city . . . What else?

DAISY. What else what?

EUGENE. What other books have you read? I mean, you don't just read books with Daisy in the title, do you?

DAISY. No. I like books with Anna in the title too. *Anna Karenina . . . Anna Christie.* That was a play by O'Neill.

EUGENE. *Eugene* O'Neill. Playwrights named Eugene are usually my favorite . . . Listen, can we sit down? I've stepped on your toes three times so far and you haven't said a word. You deserve a rest. (*They sit.*) I can't believe I'm having a conversation like this in Biloxi, Mississippi.

DAISY. You don't like Biloxi?

EUGENE. Oh, it's not a bad town . . . It's alright . . . it's okay . . . I hate it!

DAISY. I'm not that fond of it myself. Actually I'm from Gulfport. We all are.

EUGENE. Gulfport? No kidding? I know a girl from Gulfport.

DAISY. Really? Who is she? Maybe I know her.

EUGENE. Oh no . . . I doubt it. She's in the clothing business . . . Do you go to school there?

DAISY. (*nods*) Mm hmm. St. Mary's. It's Catholic. An all girls' school. I really have to move on. We're supposed to mingle. If we're with anyone more than ten minutes the Sisters get very nervous.

EUGENE. We haven't used up ten minutes yet . . . Please! I really like talking to you.

DAISY. Well . . . just a few minutes.

EUGENE. Would you like a coke or something?

DAISY. It's way on the other side of the room. You could use up at least a minute and a half getting it.

EUGENE. You're right. Let the next guy get you a coke . . . Listen, I know this is going to sound a little prejudiced, but I didn't think there were any girls in the South like you . . . I mean so easy to talk to.

DAISY. Oh, there are, believe me. Anyway, I'm not really from the South. I was raised in Chicago. My father used to work on a newspaper there. Then he got a job in New Orleans on the *Examiner* as City Editor, but he took six months off first to write a book.

EUGENE. Your father's a writer? That's incredible because that's what I want to be. Listen, not to get off the subject, but would it offend you very much if I told you that I thought you were extremely pretty?

DAISY. No. Why should it? I like it when boys think I'm pretty.

EUGENE. Do lots of boys think you're pretty?

DAISY. I hope so but they don't always say it. They get very shy around me. My dad thinks I intimidate boys my own age. I'm glad you don't seem intimidated.

EUGENE. Well, no. I told you, I'm from New York.

DAISY. . . . What kind of writer do you want to be?

EUGENE. I don't know yet. So far all I've written is a few short stories and my memoirs. I keep a notebook and write down all my thoughts and what I feel about things. I've been doing it since I was a kid.

DAISY. My father kept a journal the last few years too. That's how he got to write this book. I read that that was a very good way to become a writer.

EUGENE. Well, a few people read my memoirs and they were very impressed.

DAISY. . . . Sister Marissa is glaring at me across the room so I'd better see if someone else wants to dance. (*She gets up.*) I had a very nice time talking to you, Eugene Morris Jerome. I'm trying to remember your whole name in case I ever see it in print some day.

EUGENE. You didn't tell me your whole name in case I ever wanted to write a letter to St. Mary's Catholic All Girl School in Gulfport.

DAISY. Hannigan. Daisy Hannigan.

EUGENE. Daisy Hannigan. Great name. F. Scott Fitzgerald should have thought of that before Buchanan.

DAISY. Well, you have my permission to use it. I wouldn't mind at all being immortalized. (*extends hand*) Goodbye, Eugene.

EUGENE. Goodbye, Daisy . . . God, every time I say that name I feel like I'm speaking literature.

DAISY. You say nice things. As a matter of fact, you didn't say one wrong thing in that entire conversation . . . Goodbye. (*She goes. EUGENE watches after her, then turns to audience.*)

EUGENE. At last, something to live for! . . . Daisy Hannigan! . . . Just try saying that name to yourself and see if you don't fall in love . . . I knew I had to see her again. When she smiled at me, I had tiny little heart attacks. Not enough to kill you, but just enough to keep you from walking straight. Daisy Hannigan! Daisy Hannigan!

(*He dances off alone, Astaire-like.*
Lights up on TOOMEY's room. ARNOLD sits on the stool quietly looking at TOOMEY, who sits on the bed. TOOMEY takes a long swig from bourbon bottle. He is clearly smashed.)

TOOMEY. Have a drink.
ARNOLD. I don't drink.
TOOMEY. You will tonight.
ARNOLD. Why?
TOOMEY. (*pulls a .45 pistol and points it*) Because I say so. (*ARNOLD drinks, sputters.*)
ARNOLD. Fine!
TOOMEY. You hate the army, don't you, Epstein?
ARNOLD. Yes, Sergeant, I do.
TOOMEY. Well, I don't blame you. The army hates you just as much. When they picked you, they picked the bottom of the dung heap. You are *dung*, Epstein! . . . You don't mind my saying that, do you? Because you know that's what you are. Ding dong *dung*!
ARNOLD. If you say so.
TOOMEY. Damn right I say so . . . I say so because I have a loaded .45 pistol in my hand . . . And I am also piss drunk. If a piss drunk sergeant has a loaded .45 pointed at the head of a piece of dung that the piss drunk sergeant hates and despises, how would you describe the situation, Epstein?
ARNOLD. Delicate . . . extremely delicate.

TOOMEY. I would describe it as "fraught with the possibility of crapping in your pants." (*laughs, drinks*) I'll be honest with you, Epstein. I have invited you into my private quarters tonight with every intention of putting this pistol to your ear and blowing a tunnel clear through your head.

ARNOLD. I'm sorry to hear that.

TOOMEY. I'll bet you are . . . If I were you, I'd consider that "bad news from home" . . . (*leans in closer, meaner*) How's the contest going now, Epstein? I'll bet your ass you're sorry you ever took me on, ain't you?

ARNOLD. Some days are not as good as others, I admit.

TOOMEY. When you attack a man, never attack his strong points. And my strong point is Discipline. I was weaned on Discipline. I sucked Discipline from my mother's breast and I received it on my bare butt at the age of five from the buckle of my father's Sam Browne army belt . . . And I loved that bastard for it . . . because he made me strong. Damn right . . . He made me a leader of men. And he made me despise the weakness in myself, the weakness that can destroy a man's purpose in life. And the purpose of my life, Epstein, is Victory. Moral victory, spiritual victory, victory over temptation, victory on the battlefield and victory in a God damn army barracks in Biloxi, Mississippi . . . That's what my daddy taught me, Epstein. What in hell did your daddy teach you?

ARNOLD. Not much . . . Two things maybe . . . Dignity and Compassion.

TOOMEY. (*incredulous*) Dignity and Compassion??? . . . Are you shittin' me, Epstein?

ARNOLD. A piece of dung would never shit a piss drunk sergeant with a loaded .45.

TOOMEY. (*gun to ARNOLD's head*) Don't test me,

Epstein. I'll bury you with dignity but not much compassion . . . Why the hell do you always take me on, boy? . . . I'll outsmart you, out rank you and out last you, you know that.

ARNOLD. I know that, Sergeant.

TOOMEY. Do you know what the irony of this situation is, Epstein? Is it Eps*teen* or Eps*tine*?

ARNOLD. Either one.

TOOMEY. The irony is, Epsteen or Epstine, that despite the fact that you hate every disciplined bone in my body, you're gonna miss me when I go . . . Miss me like a baby misses her momma's nipple.

ARNOLD. Are you going somewhere, Sergeant?

TOOMEY. Didn't I just say that? Didn't I just tell you I was leaving this base?

ARNOLD. No, Sergeant, you didn't. When are you leaving?

TOOMEY. At oh seven hundred, April 3, 1943 . . . That's tomorrow morning . . . I know how much you boys are going to miss me. But I don't want anyone making a fuss or anything. No gifts, you understand. If you like, you can clean a couple of latrines for me, but that's about it.

ARNOLD. Where are you going?

TOOMEY. I am reporting to Dickerson Veterans Hospital, Camp Rawlings, Roanoke, Virginia . . . I believe, in gratitude, the army is going to replace my steel plate with sterling silver . . . That means I'll be able to hock my head in any pawn shop in this country, how 'bout that?

ARNOLD. How long will you be gone, Sergeant?

TOOMEY. I just told you, you dumb son of a bitch. I'm going to the Veterans Hospital. They don't send you back from a Veterans Hospital. You become a Veteran. You walk around in a blue bathrobe and at nights you listen to Jack Benny and play checkers with the other basket weavers . . . What I'm trying to tell you, you toilet bowl cleanser, is that my active career in the U.S. Army has been terminated.

ARNOLD. I'm sorry to hear that, Sergeant.

TOOMEY. (*holds up gun again*) Don't give me none of your God damn compassion, Epstein . . . Compassion is just going to buy you a Star of David at the Arlington Cemetery.

ARNOLD. Yes, Sergeant.

TOOMEY. They can put 65 pounds of nuts and bolts in my head, give me a brown tweed suit and a job pumping gas, I will still be the best damned top sergeant you'll ever meet in your short but sweet life, Epsteen-or-Epstine.

ARNOLD. I'm sure of that, Sergeant.

TOOMEY. One night from my room here, I heard a game being played in the barracks. I heard Jerome ask each and every man what they would want if they had one last week to live . . . I played the game right along with you and put my five bucks down on my bunk just like the rest of you. (*takes out a bill*) Here's my money. You tell me if I would have won the game.

ARNOLD. The game is over, Sergeant.

TOOMEY. Not yet, boy. Not yet . . . Alright. You know what I would do with my last week on earth?

ARNOLD. What's that, Sergeant?

TOOMEY. I would like to take one army rookie, the greatest misfit dumb-ass malcontent sub-human useless son of a bitch I ever came across and turn him into an obedient, disciplined soldier that this army could be proud of. That would be my victory. *You* are that sub-human misfit, Epstein, and by God, before I leave here, I'm gonna do it and pick up my five dollars, you hear me?

ARNOLD. None of us actually did it, Sergeant. It was just a game.

TOOMEY. Not to me, soldier. On your feet, Epstein!!

ARNOLD. Really, Sergeant, I don't think you're in any condition to—

TOOMEY. ON YOUR FEET! (*ARNOLD stands.*) ATT-EN-SHUN!! (*He snaps to attention.*) . . . A crime has been committed in this room tonight, Epstein. A breach of army regulations. A non-commissioned officer has threatened the life of an enlisted man, brandishing a loaded weapon at him without cause or provocation, the said act being provoked by an inebriated platoon leader while on duty . . . I am that platoon leader, Epstein, and it is your unquestioned duty to report this incident to the proper authorities.

ARNOLD. Look, that's really not necessary, Sergean—

TOOMEY. As I am piss drunk and dangerous, Epstein, it is also your duty to relieve me of my loaded weapon.

ARNOLD. I never really thought you were going to shoot me, Ser—

TOOMEY. TAKE MY WEAPON, GOD DAMN IT!

ARNOLD. What do you mean, take it? How am I going to take it?

TOOMEY. *Demand* it, you weasel bastard, or I'll blow your puny brains out.

ARNOLD. (*calming him*) Okay, okay . . . May I have your gun, Sergeant?

TOOMEY. *Pistol*, turd head!

ARNOLD. May I have your pistol, Sergeant?

TOOMEY. Force it out of my hand.

ARNOLD. Force it out of your hand?

TOOMEY. Grab my wrist! If you dare! (*ARNOLD leaps for TOOMEY's wrist, wrestling for the .45. TOOMEY finally allows him to wrest it from him.*) Good!

ARNOLD. Okay. Thanks. Now why don't you just try to get a good night's sleep and —

TOOMEY. To properly charge me, you'll need witnesses . . . Call in the platoon.

ARNOLD. The platoon? You don't want to do that in front of all —

TOOMEY. CALL THEM IN, SOLDIER!!

ARNOLD. (*sighs and crosses to door, opens it*) Hey guys. You want to come in here a minute. (*ARNOLD comes back in. To TOOMEY:*) This is not going to change anything between us, Sergeant. This is just as illogical and insane as before.

TOOMEY. Maybe. But it's regulations. And as long as you obey regulations, Epstein, I win. (*WYKOWSKI, SELRIDGE, CARNEY and EUGENE enter the room in various states of undress. EUGENE is in his Class A's. They all seem confused.*) Men . . . as you can see, I'm pissed to the gills and have just threatened to blow Epstein's brains out . . . Private Epstein has relieved me of my weapon and placed me under arrest. You are all witnesses. (*They look at each other.*) Private Epstein will now take his prisoner to Company headquarters to file charges and complaints . . . I would just like to add that Private Epstein has displayed outstanding courage and has carried out his duty in the manner of a first rate soldier. I am putting him up for commendation. (*He smiles at EPSTEIN triumphantly.*) I'm ready when you are, soldier . . . We're wasting time, Epstein. Let's go.

ARNOLD. I'm not going to do it. I'm not going to file charges!

TOOMEY. Remember what your father taught you, Epstein . . . Show some to a man who's going to Virginia tomorrow.

ARNOLD. (*looks at him*) . . . Suppose you just get company punishment like the rest of us?

TOOMEY. You can handle this any way you want. As long as justice is served. (*They all look at ARNOLD.*)

ARNOLD. . . . Sergeant Toomey! . . .

TOOMEY. Ho!

ARNOLD. . . . I'll drop all charges and complaints, if you give me two hundred push-ups.

TOOMEY. I accept your compassionate offer, Epstein.

ARNOLD. Thank you. On the floor — please. (*TOOMEY gets down.*) Count off!!

TOOMEY. Yes, Private Epstein. (*He starts push-ups, first slowly, then rapidly.*) One — two — three — four — five — six — seven — eight —

SELRIDGE. I don't freakin' believe this.

TOOMEY. — nine — ten — eleven — twelve —

(*The lights fade on TOOMEY's room as he continues push-ups. EUGENE steps down front.*)

EUGENE. Epstein won the fantasy game fair and square because *his* really came true . . . In a way they both won, because if for only one brief moment, Toomey had turned Arnold into the best soldier in the platoon . . . The next day Toomey went to the Veterans Hospital in Virginia and we never saw him again . . . Our new sergeant was sane, logical and a decent man, and after four weeks with him, we realized how much we missed Sergeant Toomey . . . One should never underestimate the stimulation of eccentricity . . . Daisy and I corresponded three times a week and I visited her twice in Gulfport and the most we ever did was hold hands. I was either too shy or she was too Catholic . . . Finally we finished basic training and I knew we'd be shipping out soon. (*DAISY appears, car-*

rying a small wrapped package. EUGENE smiles when she appears.) Hi.

DAISY. Hello. (*They reach out and hold each other's hand.*)

EUGENE. Your hand feels cold.

DAISY. Yours feels warm.

EUGENE. Would you like to go somewhere? Down by the lake? Or to Overton's Hotel. They have dancing till midnight . . . Or we could just walk.

DAISY. I can't. I've got to be back in ten minutes. I shouldn't even be out now.

EUGENE. *Ten minutes???* . . . Are you serious? I came all the way from Biloxi.

DAISY. I know. But it's Good Friday.

EUGENE. Isn't that a holiday?

DAISY. No. It's a Holy Day. It's the day that Christ our Lord died. We have to abstain from parties or movies or dates. It's a day of prayer and mourning.

EUGENE. So why do they call it Good Friday? It sounds like Lousy Friday to me. Ten minutes, Jesus! Sorry, no Jesus. I can't believe it.

DAISY. It's my fault. I should have told you in my last letter . . . We can make up for it next week, can't we?

EUGENE. I'm not sure I'll be here next Friday. We finished basic training yesterday. We could be shipping out any day now.

DAISY. Shipping out? To where?

EUGENE. Europe. The Pacific. They haven't told us yet.

DAISY. Overseas? So soon?

EUGENE. Well, they can't keep us here forever. The army needs reinforcements. We've already lost a private and a sergeant and we're still in Biloxi . . . Can't you stay out a little later? Just tonight? I know I'm Jewish but I

don't think Christ your Lord is going to hold it against
you personally.

DAISY. I can't, Eugene. I have to be faithful to my
beliefs.

EUGENE. What about being faithful to me?

DAISY. I have been. I haven't been to another U.S.O.
dance since we met. I just don't feel like dancing with
anyone else anymore.

EUGENE. Do you mean that?

DAISY. Cross my heart. (*She's about to.*)

EUGENE. Don't cross it. Religion is always getting in
our way. I believe you.

DAISY. I think you're a very special person, Eugene. If
you want me to, I'll write to you as often as you want.

EUGENE. Of course I do. I want you to write me every
day. And I want a picture. I don't even have a picture of
you.

DAISY. What kind of picture?

EUGENE. Do you have one where I could feel your
skin?

DAISY. If I did, I wish I had one where I could squeeze
your hand.

EUGENE. . . . I'm going to shoot my foot, I swear. I
don't want to leave here.

DAISY. I'm glad you feel the same way about me, Eugene.

EUGENE. You know I do . . . I'd have come tonight even
if I knew I only had *five* minutes with you . . . Daisy,
I—I—

DAISY. What, Eugene?

EUGENE. I want to say something but I'm having a lot
of trouble with the words.

DAISY. That doesn't sound like Eugene the Writer to
me.

EUGENE. Well, I'm not writing now. I'm Eugene the Talker . . . Daisy, I just want to tell you I — I — God damn it, why can't I say it? . . . Oooh! I'm sorry. I apologize. I didn't mean to say that. Especially on Good Friday.

DAISY. I'll say ten Hail Mary's for you.

EUGENE. You don't have to do that. They're not going to do *me* any good.

DAISY. What is it you wanted to say?

EUGENE. Ah, Daisy, you know what it is. I've never said it to a girl in my life. I don't know what it's going to sound like when it comes out.

DAISY. Say it and I'll tell you.

EUGENE. (*takes a deep breath*) . . . I love you, Daisy. (*He exhales.*) Ah, nuts. It came out wrong. It's not the way I meant it.

DAISY. I've never heard it said so beautifully.

EUGENE. What do you mean? How many other guys have said it to you?

DAISY. None. I meant in the movies. Not Tyrone Power or Robert Taylor or even Clark Gable.

EUGENE. Yeah, well they get paid for saying it. I'm in business for myself.

DAISY. (*laughs*) I remember everything you say to me. When I go home at nights, I write them all down and I read them over whenever I miss you.

EUGENE. Well, if you're writing your memoirs, keep your locker closed. I don't want to be the talk of St. Mary's.

(*We hear church bells chime.*)

DAISY. It's eight o'clock. I've got to go.

EUGENE. You didn't say it to me yet.

DAISY. That I love you?

EUGENE. No. Not like that. You threw it in too quickly
. . . You have to take a breath, prepare for it and then
say it.

DAISY. Alright. (*She inhales.*) I've taken a breath . . .
(*She waits.*) Now I'm preparing for it . . . And now I'll
say it . . . I love you, Eugene. (*He moves to kiss her.*)
We can't kiss. It's Good Friday.

EUGENE. You *have* to kiss after you say "I love you."
Not even God would forgive you that.

DAISY. Alright . . . I love you, Eugene. (*kisses him
lightly on the lips.*) I have to go.

EUGENE. Daisy! This is the most important moment
of our lives. It's the first time we're in love. That only
happens once . . . When I leave tonight, I don't know if
we'll ever see each other again.

DAISY. Don't say that, Eugene. Please don't say that.

EUGENE. It's possible. I pray it doesn't happen, but
it's possible . . . I need a proper kiss, Daisy. A kiss to
commemorate a night I'll never forget as long as I live.
(*She looks at him.*) I'll even say a hundred Hail Mary's
for you on the bus ride back . . . Okay? (*She smiles and
nods. He takes her in his arms and kisses her warmly
and passionately . . . When they part, she seems weak.*)

DAISY. I think you'd better say two hundred on the
bus . . . Oh. I almost forgot. This is for you. It's a book.

EUGENE. Really? What book? I love your taste in
books.

DAISY. It's blank pages. For your memoirs. Page one
can start with tonight. (*hugs EUGENE*) Take care of
yourself, Eugene Morris Jerome . . . Even if some other
girl gets you, I'll always know I was your first love.
(*runs off*)

EUGENE. I knew at that moment I was a long way
from becoming a writer because there were no words I

could find to describe the happiness I felt in those ten minutes with Daisy Hannigan.

(*Lights up on the coach train seen at the opening of the play. It is night and the train rattles by in the semi-darkness. The same group as we saw in the first scene are in their Class A's, stretched out on the coach seats. WYKOWSKI, SELRIDGE and CARNEY are all asleep. EUGENE is writing in his new book of memoirs. ARNOLD, once again, is sleeping in the rack above them . . . ROY's shoeless foot is practically in WYKOWSKI's mouth. WYKOWSKI slaps it away.*)

WYKOWSKI. Jesus, change your socks, will you? What is that, a new secret weapon?

SELRIDGE. I *did* change them. This one used to be on the other foot. (*He giggles.*)

CARNEY. You creeps never grow up. I'll tell you one thing. After the war, I'm not having any reunions with you guys.

EUGENE. Hey, Arnold! How do you spell "vicissitude"?

ARNOLD. You don't! Leave it out. Try for simplicity. The critics will use vicissitude in their reviews.

CARNEY. Did you guys hear about Hennesey?

SELRIDGE. What?

CARNEY. He only got three months in the can. That's not so bad. After that, he's out of this war.

WYKOWSKI. With a dishonorable discharge? He better pray we lose because no one in *this* country's gonna give him a job.

SELRIDGE. The army's nuts. They shouldn't let guys like that out. They should keep them together in one outfit. "The Fruit Brigade" . . . Make them nurses or something.

ARNOLD. You hear that, Eugene? We are listening to the generation that will inherit America. It's inevitable that one of these geniuses will some day be President of the United States.

WYKOWSKI. Listen to him, will ya? Thinks he's real tough 'cause he took Toomey's gun away. We'll see how tough he is when he hits the beach.

ARNOLD. I have to warn you, Kowski, that I expect to be very seasick on the troopship. And wherever you sleep, I'm going to be in the hammock above you.

CARNEY. How about getting some sleep *now*? This may be the best bed we see for a few *years*.

(*It turns silent as the train rumbles on. EUGENE has been writing in his memoirs. He turns to the audience.*)

EUGENE. So far, two of my main objectives came true . . . I lost my virginity and I fell in love. Now all I had to do was become a writer and stay alive . . . On that first train ride to Biloxi, we were all nervous . . . On the train now heading for an Atlantic seaport, we were all scared . . . I closed my notebook and tried to sleep . . . (*He closes notebook.*) . . . When I opened the notebook two years later, I was on a train just like this one, heading for Fort Dix, New Jersey, to be discharged . . . I reread what I wrote to see how accurate my predictions were the night Wykowski broke into my locker . . . Roy Selridge served in every campaign in France, was eventually made a sergeant and sent back to Biloxi to train new recruits. He has men doing three hundred push-ups a day . . . Wykowski was wounded at Arnheim by a mortar shell. He lost his right leg straight up to the hip. He didn't get the Medal of Honor, but he was cited for outstanding courage in battle . . . Don Carney, after six months of constant attack by enemy fire, was hospitalized for severe depression and neurological disorders. He never sings any more . . . Arnold Epstein was listed as missing in action and his body was never traced or found. But Arnold's a tricky guy. He might still be alive teaching philosophy in Greece somewhere. He just never liked doing things the army way . . . Daisy Hannigan married a doctor from New Orleans. Her name is now Daisy Horowitz. Oh, well . . . She sends me a postcard every time she has a new baby . . . As for me, I never saw a day's action. I was in a jeep accident my first day in England and my back was so badly injured, they wanted to send me home. Instead they gave me a job writing for *Stars and Stripes*, the G.I. newspaper. I still suffer pangs of guilt because my career was enhanced by World War II . . . I'll tell you one thing, I'm glad I didn't know all that the night our train left Biloxi for places and events unknown! (*CARNEY begins singing a whimsical, romantic song of the period as . . .*)

THE CURTAIN FALLS

PROPS

ACT ONE
SCENE 1: Train

5 Soldiers' equipment (U.S. Army)
Cigarettes—American 1943 brands & length
Matches
Lighters—Zippo's?
Wristwatches—Military? Tank watches? (1943)
Luggage—5 G.I. duffels, large, fully-packed (1943)
Wallets, with money, pictures, etc.
Dressing?
Candy (1943—Baby Ruth, Oh Henry, etc.)
Chewing gum (1943 brands, wrappers)
Coca-cola bottles? (1943 size & shape)
Magazines—Look, Liberty, Life
Newspapers—Sporting News, Ft. Dix News, Newark
    Eagle, etc.
Camera?
Books (Epstein)—Kafka, Melville (1959), Tolstoy,
    Dostoevski (1959)
Eugene's note book—green & white marbled school-
    book, stiff-backed
Eugene's pen—(fountain?) or pencil (mechanical?
    wood?) (Show needs *many*.)
Book of matches—1943, practical (doubled?)—(Wy-
    kowski)
General
    Dog tags—all G.I.'s
    Wristwatches—all cast
    I.D. bracelets, silver, etched
    Crosses on neck chains
    St. Christopher's medals on chain, etc.

91

SCENE 2: Barracks

6 Mattresses, single, G.I., rollable to store at foot of
    G.I. bunks (shop?) – 1943 U.S. Army
6 G.I. Army blankets – to fit mattresses (khaki? grey?)
12 G.I. Army sheets – to fit mattresses (khaki?)
6 G.I. Army pillows
6 G.I. Army pillowcases
5 G.I. duffel bags, packed – duplicates of Act One,
    Scene 1
3 G.I. Army footlockers, with trays, hasps, locks, keys
    (shop) practical
3 G.I. Army upright lockers, with locks, keys (shop)
G.I. Army non-com's clipboard (metal?), with army
    papers, forms, lists (Toomey)
Army pencils (Toomey)
Campaign ribbons, U.S. Army 1931–43 (Toomey)
    (include North African campaign, Purple Heart,
    Good Conduct, Overseas, ETO, Combat Infantry,
    etc. – costumes?
Wristwatch, for non-com (Toomey)

SCENE 3: Mess Hall

Wooden mess table, seats 6 (shop)
6 Aluminum G.I. mess trays (section E, D, or W)
6 Forks, knives, spoons – metal, G.I.
6 Metal mugs (glasses?) – G.I.
"Food," G.I. – *edible*, scrapeable onto other trays
"S.O.S." (chipped beef on toast – "greenish"?)
"Squash" ("yellow stuff")
Bottle of ketchup – practical – 1943
Salt & pepper shakers?
Sugar jars – on table, re-fillable from

Can or pitcher of sugar with spoon (large, G.I.) or spout
    (Hennesey)
Metal non-com clipboard (repeat?) (Toomey)
Non-com's pencil (pen?) (repeat?) (Toomey)
Many G.I. trays — (dressing)
Stamped letter from Arnold's DR., in envelope — to fit in
    Arnold's breast pocket (*many* — 1 torn up each per-
    formance — edible?)
Wallet, with paper money, coins — include $9.50 (Eugene)

SCENE 4: Swamp

Eugene's full field pack — 1943 G.I. — donned onstage
Eugene's carbine — 1943 M1 — with sling straps — *practi-
    cal*
5 More full field packs
5 More carbines — not practical
G.I. flare gun — dummy (Toomey)?
Sgt. Toomey's pistol — G.I. 1943 — (.45, belt, holster,
    thongs) — *practical* (fires 4 times rapidly) (+ s.m.
    cover)

SCENE 5: Barracks

Handkerchief (khaki?) (Arnold)?
G.I. towels (khaki) (6)
6 Toilet kits, G.I., with:
    Toothbrushes
    Toothpaste
    Razors (1943)
    Shaving cream or soap
    Styptic pencils
    Shaving lotion (Acqua Velva, etc.)
    Hair oils, etc.

"White creamed dots" — calamine? (Wykowsky)
Dressing for lockers, footlockers:

  Toilet articles, framed photos, shoe shine kits
  Rifle cleaning kits, butt cans, brass polishing kits,
    brushes, combs
  Como pin-up (Carney)?
  Turner, Grable, Hayworth, Garland, Sheridan,
    Darnell (pin-ups for Selridge)?
  Playing cards, magazines, books
  G.I. clothing — web belts, canteens, helmets, etc.
  Cigaretts, lighters, matches, etc.
Money (singles, fives) in wallets
Eugene's note book (duplicate)

SCENE 6: Latrine & Barracks

Toilet articles (duplicate Act 1, Scene 5) & towels (include sen-sen?)
Empty wallet (Wykowski's)

SCENE 7: Barracks

Sgt. Toomey's wristwatch
Arnold's wallet with paper money (peels off $62.00)
62 Dollars in folded bills (Toomey)
Carney's wallet with money
Eugene's watch

ACT TWO
SCENE 1: Hotel Room

2 Armchairs — worn
Table (shop)
Cigarettes, matches, lighters
Ashtrays

Selridge's watch
Dressing — floor lamp, doilies? throw rug? men's combs?
    sen-sen?
Wallets, with money?
Chewing gum (Wykowski)

SCENE 2: Rowena's Room

Four-poster bed (to fit pallet) (shop?), with:
    Crumpled sheets — civilian — blue? pink?
    Blanket
    Coverlet — civilian, worn, faded
    Pillows — civilian, with pillow cases
Dresser with:
    Mirror
    Lamp (2?) — practical
    Ashtray
    Hairbrush (practical) & comb (set?)
    Lipstick
    Powder & puff
    Mascara & brush
    Atomizer with perfume
    Hairpins
    Tweezers
    Rouge
    Make-up bag or "model's bag"?
Civilian towel (Gene)
Cigarette (Gene)
Lighter (civilian? G.I. gift Zippo?) (or matches)
    (Rowena)
2 Magazines — 1943?
Rowena wristwatch?
Clock on dresser?
Dinner bell? ("next")

Home-made cookies (tin? bag?)

Scene 3: Barracks

Eugene's note book (2nd duplicate) (Wykowski)
Carney's letter (Carney)
Kafka paperback — worn (Arnold)
(Other paperbacks?)
Playing cards — used, worn, poker
Baseball cards? Sporting News? (Carney)
Cigarettes, matches, lighters
Toilet kit, towel? (Hennesey)

Scene 4: Steps

Cigarettes, matches, lighters (Eugene, Carney)

Scene 5: Barracks

Toomey's watch (clock — to tick loud later?)
Toomey's clipboard (metal), papers, pencil, etc. (sheet
    to make notes)
Eugene's note book (3rd duplicate — page ripped out)
Toomey's Sam Browne belt (repeat), with holster (with
    thongs?)
.45 Pistol
Toomey's .45 (not practical)
Handcuffs (G.I., tricked not to lock)

Scene 6: Rowena's Room

Repeat Act Two, Scene 2
Perfume Atomizer
Paper money (tucked into Eugene's shorts)

SCENE 7: Church Basement

5 Chairs (shop)
Wall pay phone — 1943 — separate hand piece?
Small amount of coins (Carney)
Cigarettes, lighter, matches
Dressing — bottles of coke? (1943)

SCENE 8: Toomey's Room (full)

Phone — black, rotary, 1943
Bed — single G.I. cot, 1943?
Table — with phone, papers, etc.
Chair — tips over (reinforced?), (spares)
Camp stool (repeat)
Footlocker?
Wall unit (shop) with dressing — photos, books, radio (?),
    lamp (?)
.45 Pistol (cockable 2-5c, clip & bullets unloaded. Fake!
    put to actor's head!)
2 Quart bottles of bourbon, (1-½ filled)
Order sheet — to fit in breast pocket (Toomey)
Toomey's wristwatch (repeat) — tank?
Toomey's wallet, with paper money

SCENE 9: Park Bench

Park bench — 1943, outside Girls' School (shop?)
Tree? (shop)
Bushes (shop)
Old-fashioned lamppost? (electric? gas?)
Small gift-wrapped package (book of blank pages —
    opened on stage?) (Daisy)
Cross on chain? (Daisy)
Wristwatch? (Daisy)

SCENE 10: Train

Duffels, back packs, G.I. class 'A' gear for 5 (repeat)
Eugene's new memoir book (size identical to Scene 2 package)
Eugene's pencil or fountain pen (new? repeat?)
Dressing? — sandwiches, bottles, magazines, etc.?

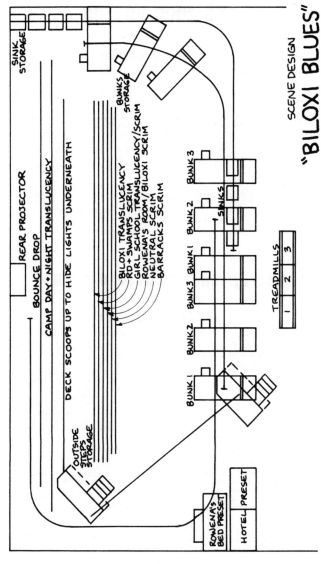

SCENE DESIGN

"BILOXI BLUES"

THE GOOD DOCTOR

NEIL SIMON

(All Groups) Comedy
2 Men, 3 Women. Various settings.

With Christopher Plummer in the role of the Writer, we are introduced to a composite of Neil Simon and Anton Chekhov, from whose short stories Simon adapted the capital vignettes of this collection. Frances Sternhagen played, among other parts, that of a harridan who storms a bank and upbraids the manager for his gout and lack of money. A father takes his son to a house where he will be initiated into the mysteries of sex, only to relent at the last moment, and leave the boy more perplexed than ever. In another sketch a crafty seducer goes to work on a wedded woman, only to realize that the woman has been in command from the first overture. Let us not forget the classic tale of a man who offers to drown himself for three rubles. The stories are droll, the portraits affectionate, the humor infectious, and the fun unending.

"As smoothly polished a piece of work as we're likely to see all season."—*N.Y. Daily News.* "A great deal of warmth and humor —vaudevillian humor—in his retelling of these Chekhovian tales."—*Newhouse Newspapers.* "There is much fun here . . . Mr. Simon's comic fancy is admirable."—*N.Y. Times.*

(Music available. Write for particulars.)

The Prisoner of Second Avenue

NEIL SIMON

(All Groups) Comedy
2 Men, 4 Women, Interior

Mel is a well-paid executive of a fancy New York company which has suddenly hit the skids and started to pare the payroll. Anxiety doesn't help; Mel, too, gets the ax. His wife takes a job to tide them over, then she too is sacked. As if this weren't enough, Mel is fighting a losing battle with the very environs of life. Polluted air is killing everything that grows on his terrace; the walls of the high-rise apartment are paper-thin, so that the private lives of a pair of German stewardesses next door are open books to him; the apartment is burgled; and his psychiatrist dies with $23,000 of his money. Mel does the only thing left for him to do: he has a nervous breakdown. It is on recovery that we come to esteem him all the more. For Mel and his wife and people like them have the resilience, the grit to survive.

"Now all this, mind you, is presented primarily in humorous terms."—*N.Y. Daily News.* "A gift for taking a grave subject and, without losing sight of its basic seriousness, treating it with hearty but sympathetic humor . . . A talent for writing a wonderfully funny line . . . full of humor and intelligence . . . Fine fun."—*N.Y. Post.* "Creates an atmosphere of casual cataclysm, and everyday urban purgatory of copelessness from which laughter seems to be released like vapor from the city's manholes."—*Time.*